THE COBBLER OF
SPANISH FORT
AND OTHER FRONTIER STORIES

THE COBBLER OF SPANISH FORT AND OTHER FRONTIER STORIES

JOHNNY D. BOGGS

FIVE STAR
A part of Gale, a Cengage Company

GALE
A Cengage Company

LIBRARY OF CONGRESS CATALOGING-IN-PUBLICATION DATA

Names: Boggs, Johnny D, author.
Title: The cobbler of Spanish Fort and other frontier stories / Johnny D Boggs.
Description: First edition. | Waterville, Maine : Five Star, [2022]
Identifiers: LCCN 2021021015 | ISBN 9781432887261 (hardcover)
Subjects: LCSH: Frontier and pioneer life—West (U.S.)—History—19th century—Fiction. | GSAFD: Western stories. | Historical fiction. | LCGFT: Western fiction. | Historical fiction.
Classification: LCC PS3552.O4375 C63 2022 | DDC 813/.54—dc23
LC record available at https://lccn.loc.gov/2021021015

First Edition. First Printing: January 2022
Find us on Facebook—https://www.facebook.com/FiveStarCengage
Visit our website—http://www.gale.cengage.com/fivestar
Contact Five Star Publishing at FiveStar@cengage.com

Printed in Mexico
Print Number: 01   Print Year: 2022

For short-story writers of years past—
Isaac Asimov, W.W. Jacobs, Dorothy M. Johnson, W.P. Kinsella,
Jack London, Conrad Richter, Jack Schaefer, Mark Twain . . .
and today—
T.C. Boyle, Jennifer Egan, Loren D. Estleman,
David Edgerley Gates, Vonn McKee, Deborah Morgan . . .

TABLE OF CONTENTS

INTRODUCTION

About the first story in this collection: For twenty years, I covered cowboy boots for a trade magazine for the Western retail industry, and also wrote a number of profiles of custom bootmakers for consumer magazines. The names Justin and Tony Lama are practically as synonymous with the American West as Stetson and Colt. My wife says I'm addicted to cowboy boots, thus the two dozen pairs I own . . .

At the annual Denver market in January, I'd find time to sit with Canadian bootmaker Tony Benattar, and we'd spend a half hour talking about the books we had recently finished. Over numerous visits, the late Dave Little and the late Eddie Kimmel of Texas, and Deana McGuffin of New Mexico—all custom bootmakers—always found time to answer my silly questions.

Years ago, another incredible bootmaker, Tennessee native Rodney Ammons—we share the same birthday (though not the same birth year)—told me about an old Hispanic bootmaker he had known. That story stuck with me for years till I finally had to write "The Cobbler of Spanish Fort." I borrowed histories of other bootmakers, and hit up Rodney to make sure I didn't screw up the boot-making process.

The rest of these stories—some new, most of them previously published, as early as 1984—are divided into parts. In the first section are stories that have won awards, including "A Piano at Dead Man's Crossing," which earned my first Spur Award from Western Writers of America.

The second part, since I am a South Carolina native with a hard-to-mask accent, contains stories from the Southern frontier. "I Am Hugh Gunter" tells about a Cherokee in the Carolinas who has been forced to pretend he is Black Dutch after the forced removal of Cherokees on the Trail of Tears. The others might be set in the South—a larger percentage of my early fiction was basically autobiographical Southern stories—but could easily be transposed to the West. Besides, Five Star published three frontier novels I set in the South Carolina backcountry of the 1700s (The Despoilers, Ghost Legion, *and* The Cane Creek Regulators), *and of all the stories I've presented at readings, "Massacre of Chest of Drawers Mountains," about a Carolina kid playing cowboys and Indians, gets the biggest response; the hero is based on a first cousin, killed in action in Vietnam in 1969. Yes, the boy narrator is pretty much me.*

The stories in "The Early Years" illustrate what I was writing when I wasn't working as a sports reporter or copy editing sports articles for newspapers. For instance, "Irish Whiskey," my second published short story, was written when about the only West I had personally seen was at Six Gun Territory, an Old West theme park in Silver Springs, Florida, that I visited while spending a week or two with relatives in the early 1970s.

In "Civil War Tales" you'll find a few stories set, obviously, during the Civil War—as have been a number of my novels, including the award-winning Camp Ford, Poison Spring, And There I'll Be a Soldier, *and* South by Southwest, *all originally published by Five Star.*

The last section, "Cowboy Stories," is included because someone emailed me and said I don't write many cowboy stories. That perplexed me. I know cowboys, I've worked alongside cowboys (enough to know I have no career as a cowboy), and I've written, I think, quite a lot about cowboys (The Lonesome Chisholm Trail, The Hart Brand, Hard Winter, Return to Red River, A Thousand Texas Longhorns . . .). *I don't write just about baseball players, crazy old codgers, and murdering outlaws.*

THE COBBLER OF
SPANISH FORT

Emilio Varela made a fine pair of boots.

No, you wouldn't know him. But there's a fair to middling chance that he made, or had a hand in making, those boots you've seen most old-timers wearing since you pulled out of Denton—you know, the ones that have been sent to a cobbler ten dozen times to get patched or resoled; the ones their wives begs 'em to toss in the trash heap. But those fellows won't even think about not wearing 'em. Because they're so damned comfortable.

Now take 'em boots you got on. What'd you pay for 'em? Hell's fire. And bought 'em right off the shelf, wore 'em out of the store? Well, they look fine. Mighty fine. Don't get me wrong, there ain't nothing wrong with a Hager boot. That's what's on my feet, too. But see mine? Hole in the crease there from bending it so many times, leather worn on the side from rubbing against the saddle, heels scarred from spurs, leather cracked, and that pull ripped off; don't know how many years ago that happened. But damned if I'll ever get rid of 'em.

Who's Emilio Varela? And what's he got to do with Big Eddie Hager? Son, let's step outside. Too stuffy inside on a day like this one. Sit under this shade tree. It's where I do my best remembering.

Big Eddie Hager, now he's the bootmaker everybody around here recollects. Hell's fire, he's the bootmaker everybody in these United States still talks about. He's been dead now for,

11

criminy, better'n twenty years, I reckon, and his kids, maybe even grandkids, is running that big factory over in Wichita Falls. Running it into the ground, if you ask me. Which you didn't. But, listen, if you drove all the way up from Dallas to get the lowdown on Big Eddie Hager for the *Times Herald,* I'm the one you come to see. Don't know how you made it down what passes for a road in that automobile. That pike was made for horses and wagons. But look there. Where my round pen stands. That's where Big Eddie set up his first shop. That's where he went into business. I was here when he stepped into the Longhorn Saloon. That bucket of blood was, let's see, right on the corner there. Yeah, that was a street corner back in the day. That little path with all the weeds was a bustlin' street. Big Eddie's shop? What happened to it? Oh, a twister plucked it up and scattered it across the Red River before the century turned. But let me make one thing clear. The first business Big Eddie went into didn't have nothing to do with boots.

Now, this place don't look like much now. Truth be told, it didn't look like much back then, neither. But Spanish Fort was the last stop on what you call the Chisholm Trail, what we called the Great Cattle Trail in the first years. Last stop, I mean, before you crossed the Red River. Which meant Spanish Fort was the place to get supplies. More importantly it was the place to get roostered. Because once a cowboy crossed the Red, there weren't nothing but saddle sores and backaches till he hit the End of Trail: Abilene, Ellsworth, Newton, Wichita, Caldwell . . . whatever it was at the time. Yep. And Dodge City in 'em later years. Some folks went by way of Doan's Store, off to the west, around Vernon way, to get to Dodge, but others stuck to this trail and took the cutoff west to Dodge. Never got to Dodge myself. Hell, I never even seen Abilene or Ellsworth.

Busted my leg, courtesy of a rank chestnut gelding just north of the West Fork of the Trinity, so Mr. Temple, bossing the outfit, deposited me here. And Drabanski, the gent who run the Longhorn, give me a job once I could stand on a crutch. Said I made one crackerjack beer-jerker.

That's what I was doing when Big Eddie Hager showed up. Showed up with his scissors, his hair tonics, his razors, and that candy-striped pole he said come all the way from St. Louis. That's right. Big Eddie called hisself a tonsorial artist. Opened the first barbershop in Spanish Fort. That's what I meant when I told you where Big Eddie's first shop was. Only leather he had in that place was his strops.

Done all right, too, this also being the last place a cowboy could get a good shave and a decent haircut before the End of Trail. But Big Eddie was making nickels and dimes, and he seen all 'em cowboys stopping over at Bianchi's. That's that rotting cabin on the other side of the Widow Munday's tomato patch. The Widow and me, we's the last full-time residents of Spanish Fort, but she's visiting her grandbabies up in Lawton this week. Piero Bianchi was a saddlemaker. Hailed from Florence, Italy. He'd make a good story for your newspaper, too. Come to New York. Joined the bluebellies at Fort McKavett before the War, and had been working for a saddlemaker in Dallas before he come up here on his own. But you didn't drive all this way to learn about him.

Well, Big Eddie saw these cowboys, trail bosses, and wranglers getting boots patched, saddlebags mended, bridles fixed, and that got him interested in changing his trade. 'Course, Bianchi didn't have no interest in teaching Big Eddie nothing that could reduce the money Bianchi was making.

Here's one thing you ought to know about Big Eddie Hager: He not only had ambition, he had will. Determination. One thick skull. He'd come over to the Longhorn, and since I was wearing only one boot at that time—my ankle and calf all wrapped up tighter than a rawhide hatband drying after a frog strangler—and he'd sit at the bar and just study the boot I wasn't wearing. Whilst he was asking cattle drovers what they wanted in a boot. And it was at the Longhorn—I was there, limping around on my crutches, filling glasses with pilsner or porter, and splashing rye in tumblers—when he started talking to this jasper riding drag for one of the outfits. I mean to tell you that he was talking that damned fool into ordering a pair of boots. From him, Big Eddie Hager. Well, that boy must've been well in his cups because I spied him handing Big Eddie a greenback, and Big Eddie wrote down some information, and then I heard Big Eddie tell that boy:

"When you come back from Abilene, after you stop here, you'll wear the best pair of boots you've ever owned."

They shaken hands, and when the jasper staggered out, I hopped on over to the end of the bar and said, "That boy paying you ten dollars for boots?"

"Twenty." Smiling, waving the greenback in my face, Big Eddie said: "I get the next ten when he picks up his boots."

"You ain't got the equipment, and you ain't got the know-how to make no pair of boots," I told him.

He sipped his whiskey. "I figure I got six to eight weeks to learn how."

See what I mean. Write that down. That's exactly what he said. Gumption. Big Eddie had a belly full.

And long about the middle of September—I was off the crutches by that time, limping, but wearing both boots—that boy come back, and it was right there in the Longhorn, where I had to pull that jasper off Big Eddie and stop him from stoving in Big Eddie's head. I give him a rye on the house to calm him down, and Big Eddie paid him twenty dollars, the ten he owed him, and the rest for the inconvenience.

Which could have—should have—stopped Big Eddie right then and there, but that wasn't Big Eddie's way. Next trailing season, this would've been '71, once the first herds started coming through, Big Eddie was taking orders for the best cowboy boots any drover could wear. He taken twenty-seven orders, or so he told me. Luckily, that jasper from the previous year must've give up on cowboying—can't blame him for that—and Drabanski and me, even Bianchi, kept our traps shut. Because we was all anticipating the fights that would start once 'em cowboys come back for their boots.

But . . . Big Eddie, he was a smart cuss. Sneaky, too. That son of a bitch had to be a Yankee. You happen to know where he come from? Nobody here ever bothered to ask.

Indiana. Hell, that figures.

This time, Big Eddie didn't even look at my boots. He cut not leather, but hair with his scissors. Still, Drabanski grubstaked him to open up Hager's Boots, which started at the store where that live oak stands. Wasn't much. Had been Belle Meade's bathhouse, but that previous owner—who sure weren't no belle—learnt right quick that having a bathhouse this close to a river where cowboys could bathe for free wasn't the best business, so he quit after a year and drifted back to Fort Griffin.

I asked Drabanksi what the Sam Hill was he thinking, but Drabanski was richer than God from all the beer and whiskey he sold, not to mention his cut from the faro dealer's take in the back room, and he said it'd be worth it to see Big Eddie get lynched. But Big Eddie hoodwinked us all. When he rode out one morning once the season started slowing down, I told Drabanski he wouldn't get to see no lynching, but Big Eddie was back within a week.

That's a damnyankee for you. Cowboys come back, paid him the ten bucks they owed him, and he outfitted 'em with store-bought boots. You look perplexed, sonny, so let me do some explaining. Big Eddie, see, he's getting twenty dollars for boots he probably paid two, three bucks for. Folks around here figured that's what killed Bianchi that August, though young Doc Gorman called it a coronary occlusion. Now before you get to calling cowboys stupid, let me point out that most boots wasn't made-to-measure back then. Oftentimes, there weren't no difference between a left boot and a right boot. You bought a pair, you pulled 'em on over your socks, and you soaked 'em in water. That's right, whilst you wore 'em. After doing that a number of times, the leather shrunk, and they fit like they was supposed to. More or less.

Nobody said nothing, because Drabanski was making his investment back, Bianchi was deader than Phil Coe, and if cowboys kept coming to Spanish Fort for boots and supplies, it was good business for all of us. Just so you know, the reason I stayed here was because I learnt that drawing beers and pouring rye was a hell of a lot an easier way to make a living than surviving rank geldings, bad weather, and ill-tempered longhorns.

In '72, Big Eddie taken over Bianchi's store. Drabanski figured this would be when Big Eddie got killed, because some cowboy was bound to figure out he'd been played for a fool, and I expect that's how the hand would have played out, but that spring was when Emilio Varela come into Big Eddie's shop. I was there, helping Big Eddie hang some leather on the walls and install this brand-new cash register so he'd look more reputable, and he was paying me two bucks for my time.

Emilio Varela cleared his throat, and me and Big Eddie turned, and the stranger started talking in Spanish. Little fellow he was, shorter than me even, in Mexican denim britches and a muslin shirt, both of which had seen some miles and years.

"What'd he say?" Big Eddie asked.

Coming from the South Llano and having worked with many a Mexican cowboy, I knowed some of that lingo, and Big Eddie knowed I knowed because that grin stretched all the way to my ears. I said, "He asks if this is the workplace of the famous cobbler of Spanish Fort." And before Big Eddie could react, I bowed in Big Eddie's direction, and said, *"Sí, este es el hombre que quieres. El Famoso Zapatero del Fuerte Español."*

'Course, the joke turned out to be on me. On account that I had to translate for both of 'em. I figured Big Eddie would send this tiny man, Emilio Varela, back to Fort Worth, which is where he said he come from, but Big Eddie was already scheming. He wound up hiring Emilio Varela for a dollar a day, to be paid at the end of the season.

That night, I got so drunk, so disgusted with myself and Big Eddie, that it's a wonder Drabanski didn't fire me. I felt sorry for Emilio Varela, felt sick that I didn't let the little Mexican know that he'd never see a dime of that money he was owed, and the next day, I up and told Emilio Varela the truth. But that little man just smiled, thanked me, and said that he knew that the Blessed Mother would look after him and his family, and me, too.

Oh, Big Eddie wasn't finished, though. Before the first herds started drifting in, he rode over to Gainesville and brung back three other men to work on the saddles and tack that had been Bianchi's business. I bet he paid 'em boys more than the cowboy wages he was paying Emilio Varela.

Well, the herds started coming through Spanish Fort, and the cowboys—even the ones who'd bought boots from Big Eddie the season before took more orders because a cattle drive is a damned good way to wear out a pair of boots. And Big Eddie, he watched with intense purpose as Emilio Varela carefully measured each cowhand's foot, right and left, using a little cloth ruler, going this way and that, double-checking his work like Mama always asked me to do and I never done. The drovers, well, they was all fascinated because this wasn't nothing like how they got boots. After it was all done, Big Eddie would write down the cowboy's name and brand he rode for on the paper on which Emilio Varela had writ down the numbers and notes that must've told him everything he needed to know. Once the first wave of herds come through, Emilio Varela let me know just what he needed.

"Maple trees?" Big Eddie asked.

I nodded. "That's what Emilio Varela says. For wood blocks. To carve the lasts."

"Lasts?" Big Eddie asked.

Shrugging, I said, "You hired him."

Some haggling followed, and I got the Widow Munday's husband—this being before she got widowed—to take over my job at the Longhorn, whilst I rode off in the late Bianchi's wagon, crossed the Red, and went maple-tree hunting in the Nations. Got no interest in becoming a lumberjack, I can tell you that much, but I come back with enough trees and watched Emilio Varela go to work.

Wasn't long before he had what looked sort of like 'em funny shoes you see 'em Dutchies wear. Only these was solid. Couldn't slip your foot in 'em. These was the lasts. Then, Emilio Varela would look at the notes he had scribbled onto the papers on which Big Eddie had writ down the names of the cowboys, and he'd trim the wood till it got to his liking. Sometimes, he'd take a little ball-peen hammer and tack strips of leather here and there.

After that, Emilio Varela cut the leather; then come a bunch of gluing, and sewing, and trimming. When I wasn't working, I'd watch him sometimes. He'd cut some saddle leather, tack it to the bottom of the lasts he'd carved hisself. Told me that was the insole, and after that, he carved a little channel along that insole's outer edges. Once that was finished, he soaked what he called the "uppers," then he pulled 'em over the lasts and tacked those uppers onto the insoles. Couldn't believe how many tacks he used, figured there wasn't no way those boots would ever get sold, but later on, he'd pulled out all those tacks, and saved 'em for the next pair of boots. I knowed Big Eddie, miser that he was, would like Emilio Varela saving all 'em tacks.

Emilio Varela set what was starting to at least look like a boot outside. Let the sun dry 'em. Providing, of course, it didn't look like rain.

After the boots had dried out, next day or so, Emilio Varela went to cutting out leather strips—called these "welts"—and, using his fingers, he sewed those through the uppers and into the leather insole, taken to whittling a couple of pieces of wood—"shanks," he called 'em—and glued those to the insoles. His oldest boy later told me that was to support the arches of your feet.

Emilio Varela went to cutting out more of that saddle leather, and using more glue. "Outsoles," that's what those was called, and the outsoles got glued onto the bottoms.

That's when Emilio Varela looked up, said a little silent prayer, and crossed hisself, because next come the dangersome part. Using a long knife, he trimmed the edges of the outsole, close to the welt. See, he was sitting on an overturned bucket at this point, holding a boot between his knees, and that knife blade, sharp as one of Big Eddie's razors back when he was barbering, would come damned close to Emilio Varela's belly—sometimes even sliding right into that leather apron he wore. I watched that once, just once, mind you, and after that, whenever Emilio Varela started on that chore—well, I went back to pouring beers and whiskeys at the Longhorn, or riding a horse to the river just to clear my mind.

Job wasn't finished, though. Outsoles had to get sewed to the welts. Emilio Varela also had to cut out smaller pieces of that leather, gluing the pieces together, stacking them to become heels, which then got glued and nailed to the boot's bottom. Once those had dried and looked good enough to pass Emilio

Varela's keen eye, he taken his rasp, and filed the edges of the outsole and heel, shaping and smoothing them before dying them, usually black or brown.

'Course, all this while, I'd been thinking certain-sure that when those cowboys come back across the Red, they'd be dragging Emilio Varela through prickly pear and filling Big Eddie with holes. Because there weren't no way in blazes Emilio Varela, little as he was, would ever be able to get no last out of any boot. See, all during this time, that last stayed in the boot. But Emilio Varela, well, he got to straining, grunting, but never no cussing, and he tugged, pulled, and damned if he didn't finally get those lasts out of the boots.

After that, he might file down a nail or two that was sticking through the insole and heels, and glued another piece of leather covering over 'em. He'd have to hammer some leather sticks—called those sticks "trees"—inside the boot tops to stretch out any wrinkles. Finally, Emilio Varela taken the boots to wash and clean till they looked fine. Once those trees got took out of the boots, that little Mexican would nod, sometimes smile, and every once in a while shake his head when one of his—rather, Big Eddie Hager's—boots did not meet the approval of Emilio Varela.

It taken a whole lot longer to see it all done than it's took me to tell you about—but Emilio Varela, well, son, it was just something to behold.

That's how it started, and I mean to tell you when those cowboys come back from all their hooraying and wild times in Kansas, and they pulled on their boots, you should've seen the looks in their eyes.

"Big Eddie," one of 'em ol' boys said, "I mean to tell you, sir, I ain't never had on a pair that fit like this in all my years."

Big Eddie, well, he knowed what he was doing. "You just tell your pards that if they want to wear the best-fitting boot in

Texas, they need to come to Spanish Fort."

Next year, they come in droves.

Which is why Big Eddie let Emilio Varela go back down to Fort Worth and bring back his family. They lived in a house Big Eddie had built—you can't see it from here, but I can take you to it once we're done talking if you've a mind to. I guess Emilio Varela's youngest boy was eight or nine, and the oldest, a girl, she'd have been in her twenties. Three boys and two girls, with the oldest girl having a husband and little boy of her own, the baby maybe one or two years old. That kid, also named Emilio, he didn't work, but the rest sure did.

Women, too. Emilio's wife, she and her daughters done the stitching, the boys doing all the other stuff, whilst the littlest ones just hauled out sawdust and scraps to the trash pile. 'Course, Emilio Varela, he worked the longest, the hardest, six days a week, and oftentimes parts of the Sabbath, too.

It was about this time that some of 'em cowboys asked if they could get a strip of leather across the tops of their boots, some wanting it red or maroon, others gray, maybe blue. See, most of the boots was brown or black, and this give 'em some color. Emilio Varela said he could do more than that, and you know how Texans are. A bunch of 'em soon wanted a white star front and center of both boots. Emilio Varela saw that done. Others wanted a crescent moon. Emilio Varela's wife cut out the stars and the moons, and his oldest boy, Rafael, he managed to stitch in the moon or the star into the uppers in what folks call, or so I hear tell these days, an underlay.

'Course, whenever Big Eddie got an order from some big rancher—like Shanghai Pierce one year, Charlie Goodnight another—he'd tell Emilio Varela that this particular boot, well, Emilio Varela had to work on it with nobody else doing no stitching or gluing or rasping. Emilio Varela, you bet your bottom dollar, he did just that, without complaint, and without no extra money from Big Eddie.

The next year was when Big Eddie got hitched. And the one after that was when he had to build a bigger place, and up and hired some of Emilio Varela's extended family and friends. The Big Factory—that's what Big Eddie liked to call it—would've been over yonder, behind the windmill. They taken the sign, the one shaped like a giant black boot with a red "H" underlay in the top, with 'em when they moved the whole kit and caboodle to Wichita Falls. Foundation can still be seen, and I bet you could find boot tacks and scraps of leather if you dug through the grass deep enough.

It was Mrs. Hager who come up with the idea to make up some sort of catalog with a measuring kit so folks didn't have to come all the way to Spanish Fort to get a pair of Hager-made boots, but it was Emilio Varela who listened to what some of the cowboys was saying, and started changing the shapes of the heels so the boots could hold a stirrup better. I'd say that come around 1880 or thereabouts. It was the very same year that this rancher from South Texas come up here with a gator skin. The belly of the big damn gator, I mean, and he pleaded—no, he *demanded*—that Big Eddie make him the fanciest pair of boots that God had ever seen. With this skin of an alligator one of his *vaqueros* had killed. Big Eddie said there's no way anyone could make a pair of boots out of that hide, and that rich rancher throwed the skin at him, cursed him up and down, mounted his horse, and rode away. Left the gator skin on the building's floor.

The Widow Munday and me got a good laugh over that one. First time we'd ever seen Big Eddie balk at the chance to make a buck.

Emilio Varela wasn't around when that fuss happened. He was in the back of that furnace making boots, making Big Eddie rich. But Emilio Varela was nearby when I happened to say, just in passing, that it sure would be nice to have boots not flopping over. Big Eddie said, "Let me see what I can do about that." But Big Eddie was looking at Emilio Varela when he said that.

You see, boots wasn't all that stiff—I mean, the tops of the boots weren't. And that Christmas, Emilio Varela presented me with a pair of boots—first ones with stitched tops I'd ever seen. Just a single-stitched thread of five oblong, sort of cigar-shaped patterns. Not fancy, but, well, pretty. Different, anyway, and that sure helped to keep the boots upright. Emilio Varela done that hisself. With finger, needle, and thread. I hear tell they use sewing machines these days. Emilio Varela handed me those boots with his pleasant smile. And Big Eddie, next day, he give me the bill for 'em boots.

Of course, the trail drives was over five or six years after that, but folks still came to Spanish Fort to get fixed up with a pair of Hager boots. Hager Boots. Let me be honest with you, son. Emilio Varela tried to show Big Eddie how to make a pair of boots from start to finish, and try as he might, Big Eddie just didn't have the knack. What he knowed, though, and what his wife knowed, was how to run a business. And Emilio Varela's honesty, his workmanship, well, that rubbed off on Big Eddie. He wasn't cheating folks no more, not trying to pull some flimflam. Hell, he was bringing in too much money then to try some joke or prank. The cattle market might have dried up in these parts, sent Doc Gorman and many others to bigger towns, but the boot-making business was like the California gold rush, I mean to tell you, here in Spanish Fort.

Of course, you know from your travels that this place ain't exactly the easiest spot in these United States to get to. I guess some big-to-do from Wichita Falls come over here the winter after Drabanski keeled over from an apoplexy. I'd taken up breeding quarter horses by then because a body couldn't make no living pouring whiskey in this country no more, and I was pretty much like Big Eddie when it come to making boots.

Emilio Varela said I wore a pair right good, but that I should leave the making 'em to him or his kids.

Well, son, you know the rest of the story. Hager Boots became about as famous as Teddy Roosevelt and Sam Houston in this country, and much of the whole world. I don't know how much that family's worth, but I reckon any Hager could buy this part of Texas with just his or her going-to-town money.

Anyhows, when the Hagers finally pulled up their roots and lit out for Wichita Falls, Emilio Varela stayed behind. He blessed his sons and grandchildren with the task of starting things over in Wichita Falls. *"Esta es mi casa,"* he told 'em. *"Mis raíces están enterradas aqui."* Yeah, this was his home, but it wasn't just his roots that was buried here. His wife had been called to Glory two years earlier.

I can take you to the cemetery if you like, but I'll ride my horse if you don't mind. I ain't getting in that contraption that brung you all the way from Dallas. Emilio, he's with her, too. Reckon he passed . . . must be nine, ten years now. When I didn't see him tending his garden, I figured to find the worst. Knocked on the door, peeked inside the windows, then went around the back of his place. He was sitting on his rocker, facing the east, cup of coffee on the side table hardly even touched.

Peaceful way to go, I reckon. Not like Big Eddie, keeling over from a stroke after all that haggling with that company that wanted to buy him out. And that was right after his oldest daughter decided to open up her own boot company, go into competition with her daddy. Well, from what I hear, Martha Jane makes a pretty good boot her ownself. Anyway, after I found Emilio Varela, I rode over to the nearest place that had a telephone, got in touch with his oldest son in Wichita Falls, then telephoned Doc Gorman, who by then was hanging his shingle in St. Jo, asked him to ride out to make sure Emilio Varela was gone 'cause that's the way folks want things done these days. And went back inside the house to let his cat out. Never cared much for cats. That's when I found 'em, sitting on the dresser.

Now, Hager Boots & Company, Incorporated, had been gone from Spanish Fort for umpteen years, but I saw the lasts and the knives, and the leather. It was the leather I remembered. That skin of the alligator some rich rancher from way down south had brung up all 'em years ago. And the boots.

Big Eddie Hager must've been rolling in his grave that day. Don't tell me how he done it, but Emilio Varela had softened that hard skin enough, shined that hide up so that it reflected like glass. Must've dyed the hide black, because it was a greenish-gray the way I recollected. The gator skin, that's what he used for the bottoms. The uppers reached up fourteen inches. The uppers was black, what they call waxed calf leather. He'd stitched the uppers with royal blue thread in a pattern that looked just like a tulip. Boots gleamed like Sir Lancelot's armor—you can write that down, too, if it's poetic enough for you and your editor.

Most beautiful pair of boots I've ever seen, and living in Spanish Fort nigh sixty years, son, I've seen me a passel of boots. But don't reckon I'll ever see anything that perfect. They was a wonder.

No, no, I didn't keep 'em. Don't know if they'd even fit on my feet. I just stared at 'em, marveled at 'em, till ol' Doc Gorman drove up.

I built the casket. And me and that ol' sawbones got Emilio Varela dressed in his Sunday-go-to-meetings, because Emilio Varela had made the Wellingtons the doc wore even if the insides was stamped *Handmade by E.J. Hager*. I saw Emilio different then, and I don't mean because he was dead. I saw the scars carved into his stomach, scars from the knives slipping while he was trimming outsoles—remember, that dangersome job I told you about—and the blades had cut through his leather apron. I also saw the permanent calluses on his hands and fingers, and the tip of one finger he'd cut off by accident, the others dotted with prick marks from millions of needles. Saw the knots and misshapen fingers. And I envisioned all the blood he had spilled for Big Eddie Hager.

"Wonder who he made those boots for?" ol' Doc Gorman asked. "Never seen any boots like that, not even in Fort Worth."

I wondered, too, but I knowed Emilio Varela hadn't made 'em for hisself. That wasn't his style. He probably just made 'em for the pure enjoyment. Boots was his life. And, yeah, me and the doc understood how much Hager Boots & Company, Incorporated would have loved to show off 'em boots inside a glass case in the center of that room that serves as a museum at their factory in Wichita Falls.

Maybe that's why ol' Doc and me put 'em beautiful boots on Emilio Varela.

He's walking those Streets of Gold in the finest pair of cowboy boots ever made on this earth.

That's fitting, if you was to ask me. Because in all those years I knowed Emilio Varela, I never once saw him wearing a pair of boots. From the time he walked down that road into Spanish Fort until the time Doc and me carried him from the rocking chair on his back porch to his bed, Emilio Varela had worn nothing but plain ol' sandals.

But, Lord A'mighty, Emilio Varela made a fine pair of boots.

* * * * *

AWARD WINNERS

* * * * *

In 2002, "A Piano at Dead Man's Crossing" won the Western Writers of America's Spur Award—my first—for Best Short Fiction. Three years earlier, I was on a cattle drive in the White Mountains of Arizona, working on a magazine profile of a ranch family. On the evening before the last day of the spring drive, a neighboring rancher told me about a piano that had been found in an old homestead in this rugged country. "Imagine," she said, "the stories that piano could tell."

The others—"The Cody War," "Umpire Colt," "Comanche Camp at Dawn," and "The San Angela Stump Match of 1876"—were Spur finalists, and "Plantin' Season" was a finalist for the Western Fictioneers' Peacemaker Awards. It's flattering to be singled out for any award, but since, to me, writing short fiction is the hardest form of prose to write, I probably cherish these awards more than others I have won. One short note about "Comanche Camp at Dawn." A friend of mine, Comanche artist Nocona Burgess, asked me to write a short story to be included in a book of his art that was to be released at the prestigious Santa Fe Indian Market. This one remains a personal favorite.

A Piano at Dead Man's Crossing

She stands in front of the plate-glass window where she has been on display for eighteen months, baking in the sun as passersby hurry down the boardwalk to buy whatever Prescott has to offer. The "Price Reduced" sign put up a week ago by the man with the reddish-gray dundrearies does no good. Few stop to even window-shop.

A year has passed since someone touched her ivories. A plump woman named Gossamer Jane had rubbed her pasty fingers over the double mahogany-veneer case and played a few bars of some minstrel song called "Oh, Dem Golden Slippers."

"The girls'll like it," Dundrearies had said. "Gossamer Jane's will be the class of Prescott."

The woman laughed and stepped away. "Two hundred is too steep. When you come down to seventy-five, lemme know."

"You'll never get it for seventy-five, Jane. I promise you that."

"We'll see," the woman said.

She hadn't returned.

Prescott booms. People come here to wash down the Arizona dust or to visit places like Gossamer Jane's. They need grub, the "law" or Doc DeWitt, maybe "a bath and a shave." No one needs an upright grand piano.

Seven and one-third octaves. Double-roll fall board and full-swing music desk. Hand-carved panels and Queen Anne trusses. Double repeating action. Nickel-plated hinge on the fall board. Ivory keys and ebony sharps. Three pedals. Eight hundred pounds. Nothing can match her in Prescott.

Some locals call her Harrigan's Folly.

A man stops in front of the window and runs long fingers through a rough matted beard. He wears a muslin shirt, stained canvas suspenders, and brown trousers caked with dried mud and drier dust. A flat-brimmed, low-crown Boss of the Plains that John B. Stetson wouldn't claim tops his narrow head, and something bulges in his left cheek as he stares through the glass. Finally, he spits a brown waterfall onto the boardwalk and walks away.

Good. He's no musician, and it's better to cook in Harrigan's Dry Goods than to be chopped up for winter kindling.

The bell over the door chimes. Dundrearies rises from his perch behind the counter and puts on his fake smile.

"Good afternoon, sir. What can I do for you today?"

"Like to see that pianer."

After recovering from shock, Dundrearies uncovers her ivories and steps back. The bearded man hesitates, then pounds a few keys and sharps that result in a groan. He jerks back.

"I'll take 'er," he says.

"Sir?"

"Said I'll take 'er. How much?"

"Er. Two hundred and eighty dollars in U.S. script. Or two-twenty-five in gold. That's a bargain, like the sign says."

Haggling should come next, but the man nods and hefts a pouch from his trouser pocket. Doesn't he know he's being cheated?

They weigh gold dust on the counter scales, and the clerk writes out a receipt. He can't contain his grin until the bearded man says, "The sign says you'll deliver anywhere in the Territory."

"Yes, sir. For the piano, that would be, oh, ten dollars extra."

"Done," says the new owner, walking to the map that hangs

on the far wall. He stretches a long arm up to the far right-hand corner of the map, then drops down, tracing a bony finger past Fort Defiance, Saint Johns, on down until he reads "White Mountains." He jabs at a place and says, "Here. You can get directions from Jake's at Springerville. How long?"

Dundrearies slowly shakes his head. "A month, maybe?"

The man hands him a couple of gold coins. "Pleasure doin' business with you."

The bell over the door chimes, and the owner walks down the boardwalk whistling "The Blue Tail Fly."

Dundrearies stares at the map.

"Shit," he says.

Wrapped in a tarp, she sits in the back of the long wagon. Branches slap the dust-covered canvas, showering the wagon bed with the scent of pine. Above the sound of the wind, the creaking of metal-rimmed wheels over malpais rock, she hears Logan, McIntosh, and Prosser—the men Dundrearies hired in Prescott—sing some song she has never heard:

> Jesus Christ! Keep movin',
> you son-of-a-bitchin' mules
> That bastard, Harrigan
> I'll kill the damn yankee
> Move, you dumb mules
> Damn your hides, I said move

The hemp rope that bites through the canvas and into the mahogany snaps from the strain as the left rear wheel slams into a hole. The tailgate opens, and she slides out, flips once, and crashes against the rocks to an out-of-tune dirge.

Prosser sings another verse of his song. Logan and McIntosh join in.

31

Don't just stand there, you scalawags
Help me get that piano back on the wagon
Set the brake, you worthless oaf
Harrigan. I'll rip his guts out
What the hell is this?
Leg's busted off. Throw it in the back
Lift on three. One . . . two . . . three

The busted leg, with its engravings now scarred and dirty, doesn't hurt. The men slide her onto her back, ignoring the rips in the canvas tarp and scratching the mahogany even more. The keys sound awful, but Prosser, Logan, and McIntosh go on with their songs. The wagon gets stuck in the first crossing of the West Fork of the Black, and the mules sing at the whip. Thrice more they cross the flowing water, then begin a harrowing climb over loose rock and dead branches until they reach the meadow and see smoke from a cabin's chimney.

"What the hell happened?" the owner asks after Logan and McIntosh have cut away the canvas.

"Mister, you try haulin' a piano up the Grapevine and 'cross Dead Man's Crossing," Prosser says. "It's a wonder that piano's in one piece."

The owner holds up the broken leg.

"I wouldn't call it one piece."

A musical voice from inside the cabin breaks a lengthy silence. "Seth, I can't wait any longer. I'm coming out."

"Come ahead, Nora."

Nora's eyes match her calico dress, sparkling. This woman doesn't belong here. Her mouth falls open. "It's beautiful."

Seth examines the piece of leg in his right hand. "Reckon we can wrap some wet rawhide around it and she'll be as good as new. Well, play her, Nora. That's what I got 'er fer."

Nora brushes dust and needles off the cover, lifts it, and hits an F. "She's out of tune, but I guess that's to be expected."

Logan has found a crate and brought it over. Nora thanks him, sits down, and plays "Lorena." Afterward, they move her inside, where Nora performs "Amazing Grace." When Seth offers to tip the Prescott freighters, Logan tells him the music has been payment enough and they'd best be on their way. Prosser calls Logan a stupid son of a bitch as they walk out the door, but Seth and Nora don't hear.

While the bearded owner named Seth lacks musical ambition, the woman, Nora, has an angel's touch. Her long fingers not only grace the ivories and ebonies, but they are strong enough to pull on the wires until a C almost sounds like a C. Maybe she'll never be tuned properly—as she had been back on the corner of Clark and Kinzie in Chicago before being shipped off to Prescott—but the music Nora makes here on this mountain up from Dead Man's Crossing sounds wonderful.

Nora knows everything, from "Barbara Allen" to "I'll Take You Home Again, Kathleen," from Johann Sebastian Bach to Stephen Foster. Nora waits until the morning light is perfect, then sits on the pine stool Seth has made. She plays, sometimes humming along, sometimes even singing. Delicately, she closes the cover over the keys and goes about her chores. At evening, she plays again, occasionally scolding Seth for leaving his coffee cup on the piano top. No one else hears her until this Sunday.

Children dance a jig outside, while the silent, smoking flutes of Seth and the other men overpower the smell of peach cobbler and elk roast. She has been hauled outside, where everyone can hear, and Nora has been coaxed to play "Oh! Susanna." Men, women, and children are still applauding as the man in buckskins reins his lathered horse to a hard stop in front of the cabin.

"Apaches wiped out Carr's command! Fort Apache's been

burned to the ground."

Seth calmly removes his half-smoked flute. "Now, I doubt that."

"Suit yourself," Buckskins says. "I'm just spreading the alarm. These mountains is about to go up in flames!"

Seth tugs on his beard after Buckskins gallops off. The men bring her inside, and pass around a clay jug. She has heard of men playing these jugs, but the only music these men make is an occasional belch.

Shortly after supper, new riders arrive, their black hair dancing in the wind as they sing and dance to another new melody in a strange language. It offends one of the ladies, who faints, while men grab long sticks like those Dundrearies sold. These instruments clang harsher than cymbals. They boom without rhythm and produce a bitter smell and thick smoke. Something thumps against the logs and splinters the shutters. One man yelps and slides down the wall while a woman—it's Nora—runs to his side and sticks a bandanna against his shoulder.

The children cry.

"It's all right!" Nora tells them. "It'll be all right!"

The other women seem transfixed by the music and excitement. The clay jug Seth has left on top of her explodes and sprays the pine walls with a foul-smelling liquid.

The children cry.

Seth works the lever of his long stick and braces himself against the thumping wall. "Play somethin'!" he shouts.

Nora looks up at him, bewildered. "To quiet them kids," Seth says. "To let them 'Paches hear our medicine. Play somethin'!" He slams the big part of his stick against his right shoulder, spins around, and strikes another harsh, loud note.

Nora crawls to her, whispering to the children, and lifts the cover. She pulls herself up, crying, and begins to play, missing a few notes, sounding terrified:

We will welcome to our numbers
The loyal, true and brave
Shouting the battle cry of freedom
And although he may be poor
He shall never be a slave
Shouting the battle cry of freedom

"Sing with me!" she repeats. And after another verse, the children obey, hesitantly at first, then louder, trying to carry their voices above songs of the long sticks. Two women join in. Even the man leaning against the wall with a sticky, crimsoned bandanna pressed against his shoulder mouths the words.

The Union forever
Hurrah, boys, Hurrah
Down with the traitor
Up with the star
While we rally 'round the flag, boys
Rally once again
Shouting the battle cry of freedom

They play and sing like that for an hour. Slowly, the men, sweaty, faces blackened, step away from the windows and door and lean the long sticks against the wall.

"I think they've had enough," says Llewelyn, someone called a Welshman.

"So have I," adds another man.

Seth smiles. "I think Nora's pianer music scared 'em off. Play us another song, gal. Somethin' we can all sing along to."

"Something less Yankee, though," Llewelyn says weakly.

Nora smiles despite her tears and begins "Green Grow the Lilacs." The men don't play their noisy long sticks this time, and those long-haired musicians outside, the 'Paches, will never return for another concert. Nor will several of the men, women, and children inside the smoke-filled cabin today.

She hasn't been played in two days. Nora is in the room where she and Seth sleep. A tired old man with a black bag has arrived. He is inside with Nora. Seth sits on the piano stool, wringing his hands.

Outside, a wolf yodels to the sky.

Seth bites his lips.

Nora's screams are painful to hear. Seth drops his head. The stranger scolds Nora. She moans. Seth looks up. Nora and the man have grown silent. Then a new tenor breaks into a strange chorus. Slowly, Seth rises off the piano stool as the stranger pushes past the bearskin that divides the cabin. This man wipes his wet face with a white rag. He looks at Seth. The music continues behind the bearskin.

"Well," the man says, "you're supposed to give me a cigar, Papa." He smiles. "You got a girl."

Seth jumps so high he almost punches a hole through the roof. He dances around the stool, hugs the newcomer, and says, "I ain't got a cigar, Doc. How 'bout somethin' stronger?"

Sometimes she misses the 'Paches and the drum of the long sticks. Visitors are few, and the wind moans frightfully. Outside stands a sheet of white, and Nora's fingers are cold on the keys as she softly follows "Oh My Darling Clementine" with "Shall We Gather at the River." The girl, Lorena, sits at Nora's side, softly kicking the base and occasionally the rawhide-covered busted leg.

Nora finishes the chorus and pushes away.

"Your turn, Lorena," she tells the girl.

"I don't wanna, Mama."

Nora smiles. "It's your turn."

Lorena hits the ivories hard, like Seth had done back in Prescott so long ago. Nora's face hardens and she slaps the girl's left hand. "Do it right," she says.

Lorena plays a gospel song, not as well as Nora. It must not please Nora because she moves away and leans against the wall, holding her stomach. She is bigger now, as she was before Lorena joined them. But she is also paler. Trembling, she collapses into a chair by the table. Lorena stops playing, turns.

"Mama?" she asks timidly.

"Go find Papa. Hurry."

Seth and Lorena wait. The man with the black bag has returned. The room behind the bearskin has become silent. No new songs from Nora. No tenor joining in for the chorus. After a long time, Black Bag steps from behind the bearskin. He says nothing.

"Lorena," Seth says. "Why don't you practice your pianer music?"

"I don't wanna, Papa."

"Please. Play somethin' for Mama."

Lorena starts with "Johnny Get Your Gun," thinks better of it and turns to "Jeanie With the Light Brown Hair." She doesn't concentrate, misses several notes.

Seth and the doctor shake hands, and as Black Bag disappears behind the bearskin, Seth walks into the whiteness outside and returns with a small wooden box, too small to carry an accordion. He, too, walks behind the bearskin while Lorena finishes the Stephen Foster song and begins "Lorena," for which she is named. As Seth and Black Bag carry the small box outside, Nora hums a new tune, a mournful wail that grows louder, like the wolf's song.

37

Lorena bites her lips, sniffling, but continues to strike the keys.

A new smell hovers in the air, thick and choking. Like a hundred fireplaces going strong in the worst winter. The sky out the window, normally a crisp, clear blue, has turned dark gray.

This is hot, much worse than baking in the window at the place in Prescott. What was that name? Pine smoke serpentines its way through the open window. Usually smoke confines itself to the fireplace and chimney.

The door bursts open. Lorena and Nora, their dresses torn and dirty, their hands and faces blackened, stumble inside, supporting the young son of the Welshman Llewelyn between them. They ease him into one of the chairs by the table.

Nora turns her head and coughs harshly.

"I'm sorry, Missus McCullough," the boy, a young man actually, says.

"Hush. Lorena, get some water. Let me see that hand, Gwyn."

They wash Gwyn's mangled hand, pink and black and red and purple, and wrap it with sheets ripped off Lorena's bed. Outside, the strange clouds have blackened. Nora suppresses another cough and rises. "You two stay here," she says, walking toward the door.

Gwyn weakly rises from his chair. "I'm helping, Missus McCullough," he says.

Lorena accompanies him. "It's my house, too, Mama," she says.

Nora smiles. "Let's go," she says.

They are gone for ages. The sky darkens more, the heat intensifies, but the wind has changed directions now, and the gray-black clouds drift away. Somewhere, a drumroll sounds. The winds picked up. And now there is a pattering on the roof, a strangely familiar sound. Rain. Yells are heard outside.

Someone breaks into a song. Some time later, the door bangs open again. Their voices are recognizable, but the soaking clothes and streaked, grimy faces and hair aren't.

Yet this is Nora, with scarred, soot-colored hands and matted hair, who sits on the stool at the urging of the others. She wipes her filthy hands on her ragged dress and stains the ivory keys as she tries a few chords.

"Play!" the man with Seth's voice says. "We gotta celebrate."

Nora looks at the ceiling. "Well," she says, "this certainly seems appropriate."

"A Hot Time in the Old Town" bangs out.

Seth, Lorena, Llewelyn, and Gwyn howl with laughter.

Lorena looks like Nora had when she first saw her: Sparkling eyes. Only the dress is white, not calico. And Nora sobs.

Seth puts a lanky arm over Nora's shoulder.

"Ain't no need in cryin', woman," he tells her.

"I'll cry if I want to," she tells him.

They have moved her outside into the pasture, where Nora plays the "Bridal March" and Seth escorts Lorena to the copse of aspens where a red-haired man waits with Gwyn. Lorena and Gwyn repeat some words, kiss, and everyone—it looks like more people than had ever been in Prescott—clap.

Later, as smoking flutes and clay jugs pass among the men, Nora launches into "On the Banks of the Wabash, Far Away," some Beethoven, and, finally, "Buffalo Gals." Lorena plays, too, "The Sidewalks of New York" and "Listen to the Mockingbird." The party seems to last forever, but finally Lorena kisses Nora and Seth and climbs into a buggy with Gwyn.

They have been on these so-called Sunday drives before, but this time they don't return. The guests leave, too, after Llewelyn, Buckskins, Black Bag, and Seth move her back inside the cabin. When Seth and Nora are alone, Nora sits on the pine stool and plays "Lorena."

After the last verse, Nora falls into Seth's arms and cries.

"A man can't make a living on one hundred and sixty acres in this country," the man with the gray derby says. "Not in this day and age."

Seth studies his coffee cup. "We've made do, Nora and me."

"Scraping by. Listen, you've got some good summer pastureland up here. Selling to my client is the way to go. You can get out of this shack, get closer to your daughter, your grandbabies. This is a new century."

"Your client needs more than my quarter section for his herd."

Gray Derby sighs. He looks across Seth's shoulders and sees her. "My God," he says, "how did you get that thing up here?"

Nora smiles. She has come out of one of the new rooms, the one Seth, Llewelyn, and some other men added a long time ago to give Lorena a place of her own. "It was a wedding present," Nora says.

"You play?" Gray Derby asks.

Nora shrugs.

"Please, may I impose?"

Nora lifts the cover and pulls out the songbook Lorena has sent. Nora plays, sings.

> No one to watch while we're kissing
> No one to see while we spoon
> Come take a trip in my airship
> We'll visit the man in the moon

Gray Derby thanks her. He shakes Seth's hand.

"Mister McCullough," he says, "I'll deny this, but if I were you, I'd never sell this land."

She hasn't been played since Nora tried "My Mother Was a

Lady" months ago. That rendition had been cut short by Nora's hacking cough.

Nora is in the room, the one with the door instead of the bearskin that had hung for so long. Seth is with her, but Black Bag, the man who usually came during times like this, is not here. It's snowing outside.

She realizes now that Nora has changed. The eyes no longer sparkle. The dark hair has turned gray, and the face is leathery and wrinkled. Nora's fingers had ached when she tried to play her.

They are both old.

Seth opens the door, softly closes it behind him, and staggers to the table. He leans on this for support. His lips tremble. His entire body shakes. He weaves around the chairs and sits on the stool he made out of the trunk of a pine. The hinges squeak as he opens the lid and stares at the ivory and ebony keys. He tries to strike a G, misses, and pounds the keys with his elbows, burying his face in his hands.

He cries.

Hours later, Llewelyn arrives. He, too, has grown old, but the two men bring a large wooden box into the room. Both men fight back tears as they carry the box outside. They are gone for a long time. Nora, she seems to understand, will not return.

Later, many people come through the door. Some of them look like those who came when the 'Paches had their concert. Gwyn is here, holding Lorena close as she sobs on his shoulder. The strangers talk among themselves. They fill the table with pies and chicken, with ham and potato salad. They talk about Nora, but no one suggests a song.

Why?

When they are gone, when Lorena has kissed Seth's cheek and Gwyn has shaken his hand, the old man again sits on the pine stool. He swallows and heads into Nora's room, returning

41

with a linen sheet. This is draped over her.

She will sit like that for years.

Heat follows cold. Cold follows heat. Verses and refrains are repeated, but no one plays her. She has forgotten so many songs from sitting uselessly underneath her shroud. Rats have chewed on the rawhide patch so that her busted leg has almost fallen off.

"Seth!" a man sings. "Seth McCullough. It's Pryderi Llewelyn. You there?"

There is no answer. The door opens. Relying on a cane, Llewelyn hobbles inside. He glances across the room and moves to Nora's place, where Seth went in some time ago. Llewelyn slowly opens the door, closes his eyes for a minute, and stumbles inside. A few minutes later, he is back out, shutting the door. He inhales deeply.

Another man, a stranger, comes inside. Llewelyn looks at him.

"He's gone," Llewelyn says.

The man nods. "Damned shame. Reckon he was up in years, though. Hell of a long life, especially up here."

A new sound putters outside. The door opens. Gwyn Llewelyn opens the door, mopping his older face with a calico rag. Two bronze-skinned strangers, equally sweaty, follow him inside. Outside stands a weird wagon, rubber tires instead of spoked wooden wheels, and no horse to pull it.

Lorena walks inside. Two dark-headed boys follow her.

"That was an adventure," one says.

The other chimes in. "Reckon we'll get that many flats on the way down, Daddy?"

Gwyn is too out of breath to reply.

Lorena pulls the dirty sheet away and drops it on the floor.

"A piano!" the second boy exclaims. "It's a piano!"

"How did it get up here?" the first child asks.

"Your grandpa had it brought up for your grandma when they were first married," Lorena says. She lifts the covering, rubs her fingers across the keys. "Out of tune," she says, "but I guess that's to be expected."

"What happened to that leg?" the first boy asks. "It's all busted up."

"It's perfect," Lorena says.

"Go outside and play," Gwyn tells the youngsters. He turns to the bronzed men. "Y'all get the truck ready."

When they are gone, Gwyn puts his right hand on Lorena's shoulder.

"Honey," he tells her, "this is no good. We had a hell of a time getting up here in that truck. We'll never make it down with that old relic."

Lorena pulls away from him. "You promised," she tells him.

"But . . ."

"But nothing. My father had this brought up more than fifty years ago. Mama taught me to play on this. She played it on our wedding day in case you've forgotten. We've sold the land. I'm not selling this."

Gwyn shakes his head. "We'll never make it, Lorena," he said.

Lorena smiles. "We'll make it." She plays "The Flying Trapeze." Gwyn walks outside and serenades the bronze men.

> We'll throw a tarp on the bed
> And wrap another over her
> This is a family memento
> And I'm not paying you to be careless

It's a hell of a way across Dead Man's Crossing
And on to Springerville in this piece of junk

Wrapped in a canvas tarp, she stands on the back of the strange wagon, baking in the sun. Lorena and Gwyn sit up front in the metal cab of the puttering wagon. The bronze men and the two boys rest in the back, staring at her.

Humming a polka, the horseless wagon lurches forward, turns around, and heads toward the first crossing on the West Fork of the Black. She doesn't know where she's going—Phoenix, she has heard one of the bronze men say—and she will miss Nora, Seth, and the log cabin where she has been played for so long.

Lorena will be good to her, though. Nora saw to that. The wagon groans as it awkwardly fords Dead Man's Crossing. Gwyn is lucky. He should have been here when her banks were full, back before the 'Paches sang harmony and the men played their long sticks.

One of the boys begins whistling a song. The other joins in. The bronze men smile.

She doesn't know this song.

But she will learn it.

THE CODY WAR

January 10, 1917
Denver, Colorado

Shock slaps her like the brutal wind, and she quickly looks away, focusing on a frosted pane of glass, anywhere but the bed. She can picture Boy Scouts on the porch, freezing but determined to help the old scout and his family. Can visualize reporters on the death watch, can almost smell their cigar smoke and whiskey-laced coffee. Can see Harry Tammen, that heartless lout, rubbing his gloved hands, joking with ink-spillers, pretending to be friend, philanthropist, when ruination is what he sows for others to reap.

Sobs sound behind her, a moan from her sister-in-law, and whispers, but she can't make out any words, which sound as if they are coming from the bottom of an Arizona well. From behind, the priest's hand squeezes her shoulder, while Cody Boal kneels beside her, kisses her cheek. "Grandma?" he mouths.

She shakes her head. At least, she thinks she does. Maybe she can't move.

Low voices finally reach her. *He's gone . . . An era has passed.*

Her head jerks toward the men as they test their quotes for reporters—speechifyin', Will would have called it—and she snaps, "Why don't you just say, 'Now he belongs to the ages,' you damned fools!"

Silence. They stare at her, before quietly filing out to the parlor and kitchen. A door closes; she's alone.

45

She finds him again, chilled by the sight. Tentatively, she forces her heavy body out of the chair, weaves to the bedside, takes his cold hand in her own, and remembers the last time he shocked her so.

July 28, 1910
North Platte, Nebraska
"What the blazes are we doing here?"

"Aunt Irma said to bring you," his grandson answers, setting the brake and jumping from the spring wagon to help the Honorable Colonel William F. Cody down. Though only fourteen, Cody Boal's old enough to understand his grandfather is well in his cups, sure to fall face-first into the dirt without a steadying hand.

"Welcome Wigwam," the old man says. "That's what I called it. Well, she sure didn't make me feel welcome last time I was here."

"I know."

He stumbles against the child, pushes back to lean against the wagon.

"Locked herself in her room, she did. Not a word, not even a good cussin' would she give me. I went up and begged her to at least open the door. Three times I done it, and Buffalo Bill ain't a beggin' man. Not a word. Not one damn word."

"Aunt Irma said to bring you."

"Irma." His breath stinks of rye, and it's not ten in the morn. "She's a good daughter. So was your ma, God rest her soul." Grandfather runs fingers through grandson's hair. "And you're a top hand."

"Thank you, sir." He leads the old scout up the steps, opens the door, guides him inside.

Irma stands in the parlor, wringing her hands, biting her lip.

"Papa," she says, her voice quiet, and gives him a peck on the cheek.

"Thought I was goin' to the ranch," he says. "I could use a rest."

"Yes," his daughter says, "but . . ." She sighs.

He straightens. "Lulu? Has something happened to your ma?"

Her head shakes nervously. "She's . . . come inside." Taking him by the hand, she leads him to the family parlor, where he bristles at the sight of his wife, sitting on the oak divan, reading the *Telegraph*, and he bellows, his words too slurred for either Irma or her nephew to understand.

Seeing him, Louisa Frederici Cody tosses the paper aside, bolts out of her chair. "What's he doing here?" she demands.

"You two need to talk things out." Irma has found her voice, surprisingly forceful. "And don't come out until you've done it." With that, she is gone, leading her sister's son to the porch. Once the door slams, husband and wife stare at one another from across the room.

"You're drunk," she says.

"I've had my mornin' bracer." He looks across the room, finds the brandy decanter. *And I'd like to have another.* He starts to remove his hat, but when she barks at him, asking if he has a head cold, he leaves it on. *That'll show that ol' witch.*

"Well, why are you here?" Lulu asks. "To torment me more? Shame me? Why aren't you at your lovely Scout's Rest Ranch with all those friends of yours." Contempt laces her voice.

"Weren't my idea, woman. 'Specially after the welcome I got in March."

"What did you expect, you old fool? You were in your cups the whole time. And it was you who tried to divorce me! My parents . . ."

He rolls his eyes. He has heard that before. *They're spinnin' in their graves.* Sounds like that melodramatic Buntline at a temperance lecture when she speaks of that shame, that agony, heartbreak. Criminy, he had been trying to do her a favor. This wasn't a marriage. Hadn't been for some time, and he would have been shuck of her except for that judge. Wouldn't grant the divorce, nor would the court allow a new trial. That had cost him, damn near broken him, and it had been, what, four years ago? Tormented her? Shamed her? What about him?

He glares at her, a stout—hell, *fat* is the word—woman, short and stooped, with gray hair put up in a bun, clad in an ill-fitting dress and sandals in boot country. A hard-rock woman with a cast-iron heart. Sure not that charming, beautiful girl he had wooed back in St. Louis all those years ago.

"Well, you got your wish, Lulu."

"It wasn't my wish, Will."

He turns to go, but sags at the parlor entrance. He'd have to walk past his grandson and Irma, waiting outside. Be like runnin' from a fight, and Buffalo Bill never retreats, if you believe the dime novels or his Wild West show.

So he whirls, waving a finger at her. "You ain't been a wife for years, woman."

"And what kind of husband have you been? Consorting with strumpets!"

"What? You mean them actresses?"

"Whores!" she hisses.

That had been a disaster from the get-go—*Get-go?* she thinks. *Now I sound like the fool.*

It had been Buntline's idea. Ned Buntline, or Edward Zane Carroll Judson. Take Buffalo Bill, King of the Bordermen, transform him from scout to thespian. "You don't know the difference between a theater cue and a billiard cue," she told him, but he wouldn't listen. He never listened. "You'll make a fool of yourself, Will."

"I'll make us rich," he answered.

So they went to Chicago in the winter of '72, and he had played the fool, a mighty big one, stumbling over his lines when he didn't forget them. Critics panned the play, rightfully so, but performance after performance sold out. People couldn't get enough of the West back East. Chicago . . . St. Louis . . . Cincinnati . . . Philadelphia . . . Boston . . . Washington City . . . New York. Scouts became celebrities on stage and off. The reaction struck her dumb.

Of course, he had to bring his friends along. Buffalo Bill had to share the glory with his drunken troupe of bitter merry men. First, Texas Jack Omohundro, then that man-killing Hickok, later Captain Jack Crawford. Yet Will had made the family, if not rich, at least comfortable, and he had gotten them out of that hellhole frontier to civilization, with homes in Westchester and Rochester. Nice homes . . . until the . . . tragedy.

"Criminy," he's saying, "that was nigh forty years ago."

"You embarrassed me," she tells him.

She starts to stand, to head upstairs to her room. She'll lock herself inside again, until that walking whiskey vat takes his leave. She sinks back, however, her legs suddenly weak. She can't . . . not break Irma's heart, not her grandson's. *They're all I have left.*

The fool's speaking again. She looks at him, rolls her eyes.

"If you mean that time I called you out from the balcony . . ."

She hasn't forgotten that, although she can't remember the city.

He had just killed about twenty "supes," the low-paid actors pretending to be savage Indians, and for the umpteenth time, couldn't remember his lines. Usually, when that happened, he'd just start slaughtering Indians again, but they were all scattered about stage left and stage right, playing dead, and when he looked up, his face frightened, he found her in the balcony. "Mama," he cried out, "what a horrible actor I am!"

The audience loved it, clapping, whistling, cheering, then forcing her to come on stage and take a bow. "Say a few words, Mizzus Cody!" they demanded when she stood beside the show's star at center stage, but she found herself speechless, terrified, and he pulled her close, telling the crowd, but mostly her, "You see what hard work I do to support my family."

Strength returning to her legs, she pushes herself out of the divan, waves a finger in his face. *Talk things out, Irma says. Well, I'll tell that old mule a thing or two.*

"That's not what I mean, and you know it. I saw you kissing those women . . . in our hotel! With me there, with your children there. I would not be shamed so. That's why I left you, wouldn't travel with you anymore!"

"I was rehearsin', Lulu."

"Horseshit."

A long finger jabs back at her. "There. You lied! Proof you lied in court. You said you never used profane language. Your friends said you never used profane language, but you do, Lulu. You do!"

"You'd drive anyone to it. That or the bottle. Or both. You and that sorry lot you call friends. Anybody with a sad story or not a cent to his name. All he had to do was say, 'We scouted together.' Or 'We freighted together.' Or 'I was in the Army with Carr.' Or, by jingo, 'We met on a stage once.' Maybe even 'I just read one of your stories!' "

"Man who'd turn his back on a friend ain't a man," he says.

"And you'd never turn your back on a bottle, Will Cody!"

"Well, all I did was kiss actresses, either rehearsin' or celebratin' a performance. Ain't like I was ever untrue to you.

And I ain't gonna say I'm sorry for bein' kind to stranger or friend, 'specially one in need."

"Even Hickok!"

He looks dismayed. "You liked Jim."

"I tolerated him. Like I tolerated all those drunken sots you brought to our home."

He hadn't known her when he first met Hickok. He was just a kid of twelve, freighting for Majors and Russell, barely knowing one end of an ox from another, fetching anything for that bear of a man with Lew Simpson's train until the brute pushed him too far.

"Fetch that corncob, boy, and come with me to wipe my arse."

"I'll do no such." He braced himself for the whipping sure to come.

"You'll do what I say, or I'll leave welts on your back and arse. I'll make you bleed, boy, bleed and hurt."

When he looked for help, finding no friendly eyes, the skinner—he had long forgotten the villain's name—knocked him off his seat on the ox yoke, stood, and kicked at him. Will scrambled to the fire ring, found a cup of coffee, flung the hot liquid into the man's face.

The teamster screamed, but only briefly. Wiping his eyes, he charged, a maddened bear. Will figured he'd be killed certain-sure, when towering Jim Hickok stepped in and slammed the attacker to the ground. "Lay a hand on that boy again, and I'll put a pounding on you that'll take a month of Sundays to get over."

He eyes the brandy, runs his tongue over his lips, and glares back at Lulu. "I won't apologize for havin' Jim Hickok for a pard. Not ever."

"Pard? He quit on you when he was tryin' to be an actor in your Combination. And how many times did you have to go his bail, or give him spending money because he was broke? Money you were supposed to send to us. Your family."

"I ain't gonna apologize for havin' Jim Hickok for a pard," he says. "He saved my bacon, more times than once. Freightin'. Ridin' for the Pony."

"Pony! You never rode for the Express, Will, unless you count being a messenger boy for Majors. And neither did that assassin. All he did was muck stalls before he murdered those men in Nebraska."

"Freightin'. Ridin' for the Pony," he repeats, ignoring her slander. "And fightin' redskins."

Laughing, she falls back on the divan. "Indians? My Lord, Will, you killed more Indians on your Wild West than on the Plains. How many did you bury in Europe?" Her cackle slices him to the quick. "There didn't have to be a Wounded Knee, Will. General Miles should have just sent all the Sioux off with you. They'd all be good Indians, then. Dead of rot and consumption and infection. Probably embarrassment."

He moves to the bottle. "There wouldn't have been no need for that fracas at Wounded Knee had they allowed me to arrest Sittin' Bull," he says. His hands stop short of the bottle. Her words stop him.

"You were too drunk. Remember? A good thing, too, or you both would have died, you and that heathen, and what fun the newspapers would have had with that."

"I could have saved him." His eyes shut, and he sees the old Sioux again, sees him babying Annie Oakley as if she were one of his grandchildren. He sees the trained horse he had given Sitting Bull when he left the Wild West, pictures the fine stallion rearing while the gunshots fired by Metal Shirts kill the great holy man. "Could have stopped all that bloodshed. At Sitting

Bull's camp, at least. He was a friend."

"The problem with you, Will, is that you believe all your managers tell you. First Buntline, then John Burke. Salsbury. Cooper. Ingraham. Biggest liars ever, next to you."

"Maybe if you had ever believed in me, woman."

That silences her.

She had believed in him once, hadn't she?

Here was this dashing young soldier, quite handsome, with dark eyes that shined so bright. They met in St. Louis, shortly after the end of the Rebellion. Their courtship began as a joke. A cousin brought Trooper Will Cody to her house, and they began talking. Uncouth, but charming—quite a horseman, they said—and then he had suggested a joke. A suitor was calling on her that evening, and Louisa really did not want to accompany that cad to the symphony, so when he knocked on the door, she had introduced William F. Cody as her betrothed.

She never saw the suitor again, but Will Cody became a fixture on her doorstep, and when he asked her father for her hand, she felt excited. They married on March 6, 1866. He was twenty; she almost two years older, and had never been outside of St. Louis and all its splendor.

Immediately afterward, she stepped into Hell.

Two days out of St. Louis on the Missouri River steamer, she fainted in his arms when some rough men threatened to kill her husband for being a jayhawker. When they reached Salt Creek, Kansas, he showed her the hotel he planned on running, as decrepit a building as she could ever imagine, not fit for a wharf rat. He proved a mighty poor businessman, always would, so he left to scout for the Army. He wasn't there when Arta was born that December. He wasn't there when any of the babies came, and barely around before or after. Long enough to plant his seed and say goodbye. She spent more time in St. Louis with her parents than in Kansas or Nebraska with her husband. Soon, she preferred it that way.

In 1867, Goddard Brothers Company hired Will to provide twelve buffalo a day for the Kansas Pacific crews. It paid $500 a month, if he lived, and she saw him even less. He mailed some money home, spent more on whiskey, gave plenty to his lowly friends, and invested whatever he had left. Those investments never paid off. Will had better luck betting on horses than on land, and he had little luck with horses, and none at cards or dice, certainly none at choosing business partners. He did have success with the Army, scouting, especially after killing the Cheyenne leader Tall Bull at Summit Springs. That's how he had met up with Buntline, and the writer had made Buffalo Bill Cody a man of legend, even if those early stories had their roots in Hickok's depravity rather than her husband's.

"And I killed Indians." He sounds childish, but that's what he really is. A child. "Killed me aplenty. But I made a bunch of friends with the red man, too."

"Yeah," she says, mocking him. "You killed plenty, Will. You shot Tall Bull from ambush."

"Got a damn fine horse, too."

"And then . . ." Well, she can't speak of that other one.

"Then what?" he demands, not understanding. "What? I was out riskin' my hair, woman, riskin' it for you and our country. And afterward, after I became Colonel William F. Cody . . . Good Lord, woman. I've met heads of state. You see this diamond stickpin?" He points, but it's missing. Probably lost it, or gave it to some saloon beggar. Or he's so drunk he has forgotten he's clad in buckskins and not a fancy broadcloth suit. "I had Queen Victoria ride in the Deadwood stage. All these years with my Wild West, you could have come with me. You could have seen the world. You—"

"Maybe by then I was just used to being left alone!"

"I done it all for you. You and the little ones."

"You did it for yourself, and your own vainglory!"

His hands grasp the decanter. She thinks he might hurl it at her, but he releases it and whirls, ripping off his hat, tossing it to the floor. His horsehair wig falls with it.

She almost laughs.

He looks like the old fool he truly is, his once-flowing locks reduced to sweaty remnants resembling something on a mangy cur—though mustache and goatee remain thick and white—dressed in absurd boots up to his thighs and buckskins with so much beadwork the outfit must weigh more than a knight's suit of armor. It's an improvement, she thinks, mayhap over that hideous velvet suit of the *vaquero*. She closes her eyes to dam the tears, wishing she had never thought of that costume.

"I never wanted to be away!" he's telling her. "I done it all for you and the little ones. It broke my heart, you know, broke my heart when Kit died. Soon as I got word, I left the show, took the train home, only to have my son die in my arms."

There. It's finally out.

"*Our* son, damn you! He was *our* son. And he died in *my* arms, not yours!"

"Mine . . . I got home—"

"You weren't there, Will! Till after Kitty died!"

He grips the mantel for support, glances at his hat and hairpiece, and staggers to the divan. Suddenly she's afraid, but she sees the tears welling in his eyes, and he collapses beside her, trying to remember, to sort it out.

It was spring, April, 1876. The Combination had opened in Springfield, Massachusetts, performing *Life on the Border* with Jack Crawford when the telegram arrived. Joe Arlington, an actor with the Combination for years, handed him the telegram during the first act.

"KITTY HAS SCARLET FEVER. DESPERATE. COME HOME QUICK. LOUISA"

That image remains engraved in his brain forever. Over thirty-four years, not one day has gone by that he hasn't seen it.

She tells him, her voice a hoarse whisper. "You just listened to Burke and those others until you finally convinced yourself you were there."

"No." He shakes his head. *No. But . . .*

"Go on, Will," Major Burke said, but he stubbornly shook his head. "After the first act." Somehow, he made it through, then raced out of the opera house, still in his *vaquero* suit, ran to the depot. Old Moses met him at the Rochester station, driving him home without a word. Kit died on April 20, five years old, apple of his eye, his only son. Kit Carson Cody.

Yet he can't see him holding the boy in his arms. He looks at Lulu for help, but her face is blank, unblinking eyes boring holes into the wall. He thinks back to that horrible night, hearing the clock's chimes, remembers writing the letter to Julia after Kit was called to Glory, remembers checking on Lulu and the other little ones, all sick, all heartbroken.

Why Kit? he wrote his sister, wiping tears as he sat alone in the library. He tried to make himself believe Kit had crossed the Jordan, was waiting for them on that better shore, but he wasn't sure he believed it. Wasn't sure what he believed anymore.

"You weren't there," Lulu snaps beside him. "You weren't here when Orra died, either. Or with Arta when she . . . Well, at least you were decent enough to see your son planted. Then you went back to your actresses. And you left me, and your daughters, to grieve alone. You couldn't help us, just yourself, your career. So you went back to tread the boards, and then avenge Custer!"

It had been a bad year. First Kit. Then Custer. Later Hickok. All dead. He had left, too, after the season ended in June, but not to avenge Custer. Autie was still alive then, and Will wouldn't learn of the Little Big Horn until he was scouting in Nebraska. When Wesley Merritt read him the report, he passed the news on to the troops. "Custer and five companies of the Seventh wiped out of existence."

But why had he taken the train West to join the Indian fight in the first place, to put down the Sioux and Cheyenne? Why had he not changed out of that *vaquero* suit of black velvet with silver buttons he had worn on stage in Wilmington, Delaware, and elsewhere during the season?

"This is what I do," he told a newspaper editor, "when not acting. I'm a scout. And the Fifth Cavalry needs their chief of scouts."

Duty? Or was he running, running from Lulu and poor Kit Carson Cody? Running from his breaking heart? Somehow discovering who he really was.

The fight came up quickly, but, by thunder, he didn't kill Yellow Hair from ambush, not the way he had shot Tall Bull back in '69. He wasn't the first to see the Army couriers, but he did detect the Dog Soldiers pursuing them. "God have mercy," General Merritt said. "Those poor bastards don't know the savages are after them."

So Merritt ordered him and eight troopers to rescue the white men. Spurring his rangy gelding, whipping the Winchester from its scabbard, he soon outdistanced the soldiers.

He spotted the Dog Soldier—Yellow Hair he would learn—

raise his own rifle as soldiers and Cheyenne, now yipping like coyotes, charged. Reins in his teeth, he lifted his Winchester, found his target. Their weapons spoke at once, and his horse stumbled, pitching him into the sand.

He rolled, levering the rifle, seeing that his shot had killed the Cheyenne's horse. Yellow Hair had already recovered, but his second shot flew wild. He took his time, let out a breath—the way Jim Hickok had taught him—and shot the Indian in the head. Then he was running, screaming curses, unsheathing his knife. He slid beside the dead Dog Soldier, gripping the greasy black hair. He didn't know why he said it, didn't plan it, but he worked the knife and raised the gory trophy, yelling triumphantly as troopers galloped past in vain pursuit of the fleeing Cheyenne.

"The first scalp for Custer!"

"You just had to leave me," Lulu says softly.

"I reckon." His words come out more as a sigh.

She buries her face in her hands and wails. When her head lifts, she turns to him. "And then you had to mail your . . ." She shudders. "Mailed it home, Will? For the love of God."

"I wrote you a letter."

"The box showed up first. I opened it and saw the scalp. The flies, crusted blood. I fainted, Will."

Yet she's laughing now, and he sniggers a bit, too.

"Reckon it was dumb of me."

Their laughter fades.

"I miss our children," she blurts out, and the dam bursts once more. "Kitty . . . Orra . . . Arta. Irma's all we have left."

"I miss 'em, too." He starts to reach for her hand, but pulls away.

The ache is leaving him. Perhaps he's just sobering up.

"It's the leavin'?" he says, his voice suddenly sympathetic. "Is that what hurt you so?"

"And your drinking."

She makes her tears stop. She has always been strong, well stronger than he would expect for a spoiled rich girl from St. Louis who had married some wild, fatherless boy who came of age in the wilds of Kansas.

He offers her a handkerchief. To his surprise, she takes it.

"I can stop the drinkin'," he says.

"You cannot," she barks sharply.

"Hell I can't," he retorts. "I'm Buffalo Bill."

Besides, them old pill-rollers have been hammering at me for years now that the John Barleycorn would kill me. Maybe I should cork the jug. God knows, I've spilt more whiskey than most men ever seen.

"I guess I ain't been much of a husband, Lulu. Probably was never cut out to be one, way I grew up. Guess I just liked the notion of bein' hitched."

"You said as much during our . . . our divorce proceedings." The bitterness has returned, but he'll parry it.

"Yeah, and I'm sorry for that, and all the torment I put you through. But I can't stop the leavin'. Owe it. I owe too many folks."

"I know that. The Wild West. Buffalo Bill's Wild West. I never understood the fascination."

"Me, neither."

Although he had, and he had learned. By the winter of 1876, he was performing on stage again, *Red Right Hand, or Buffalo Bill's First Scalp for Custer,* wearing that *vaquero* costume again and displaying Yellow Hair's scalp and other spoils of war in opera halls across the East. He had become the showman. Westerner at heart. Showman by nature. He discovered that about himself along Warbonnet Creek.

So he had returned East, and later ventured across the world. He envisioned, not a play, but an outdoor spectacle of the West.

Since '83, when he lost little Orra, his traveling exhibition—now Buffalo Bill's Wild West and Pawnee Bill's Far East—had made Buffalo Bill Cody's name recognized across the globe. Ironically, Lulu had fled West, back to the frontier she had loathed, to the North Platte to bring up their family, later to hold Orra's hand as she died at age eleven, to become the recluse, hating him whenever he stopped in for a visit at the Welcome Wigwam—his stupid name—or Scout's Rest Ranch.

"I got my faults."

"You're generous, Will Cody, kindhearted to strangers, children, dogs, horses, old people, even those red savages. Maybe I shouldn't see that as a fault, but I do. Maybe I'm selfish."

"You brought our kids up right. Orra, Arta, Kit . . ."

When his voice breaks, she reaches toward him only to pull back her hand, whispering, "Don't, Will. I can't . . ."

"We got family, Lulu." He has recovered. "Still . . . But . . . Well, when I was here in March, when you wasn't talkin' to me or havin' nothin' to do with me, well, I wanted to ask you to come with me. Tour with me. I'm askin' you again, Lulu. I promise you I won't put you on the spot like I done that time on stage."

"Why? Why now?"

"For that family, Lulu. They want it. That's why Irma had us meet like this. Fight it out. Well, I'm plumb wore out from fightin' you. I surrender. Let's bury the tomahawk, sign the treaty."

"You can't change, Will."

"You can't neither."

Silence. She rises and moves to the window, pulls back the curtain, closes it, steps back. "I guess we do owe it to them."

He shoots out the divan like the twenty-year-old given

permission to marry the girl he adores, not the sixty-four-year-old buffoon, making a beeline for the brandy.

"Let's have a drink, Lulu. It'll be the peace pipe. War's over."

"You're incorrigible, Will Cody."

"Damn right. Buffalo Bill's a man of his word." He fills two glasses.

She approaches him, tentatively takes the glass. His clinks against hers.

"And it's my last drink, Louisa."

January 10, 1917
Denver, Colorado
He lived up to his word, too, she remembers, alone in the room with her husband. Lived up to it despite the hardships, losing Scout's Rest Ranch, losing just about everything, even his name, his show, perhaps his soul to that bastard Tammen.

Now it's over.

She feels it then, shocked by it, reaching up with a tentative finger, curiously tracing the trail the tear leaves as it rolls down her cheek. She squeezes the cold hand, hoping it will respond in kind, but when it doesn't, she chokes out a sob, maybe a groan, and she wonders:

Did she really love that old reprobate, or does she merely hate him for leaving her alone one last time?

COMANCHE CAMP AT DAWN

This is what the white men at Fort Marion said of the Comanche called Nocona:

"He was a bloodthirsty savage, an unrepentant heathen, and a malevolent fiend—but the son of a bitch could paint."

In the year the white men called 1875, the bluecoats lined up Nocona and other People—"ringleaders," they were called, those most responsible for the Red River War—and four drunken soldiers walked down the line, picking out who would go to Florida, and who would remain at home, or what had become their home on this reservation near Fort Sill. It was not just The People being punished. The white men would send Cheyennes, Kiowas, Arapahos, and even a few Caddos far away. And these bluecoats were so stupid, they even picked a few Mexican captives to be prisoners, too. Well, they once had been Mexicans until The People or their allies, the Kiowas, had adopted them. In all, seventy-two "belligerent red devils," including one Cheyenne woman and several wives and children, took the long journey to an ancient fortress once called Castillo de San Marcos. To rot away.

At this stone fort on the Atlantic, the soldier-chief named Pratt forced all of his "wards" to have their braids cut, and then gave them soldier pants and soldier blouses to wear. When Nocona returned to his dark, damp, stone cell, he cut off the legs of the pants, tossed away the crotch, and tied the blue wool on as leggings. The navy blouse he wore, although he removed the brass buttons for trade later.

He hated this place. He longed to see his wives, his sons, his country. He missed the mountains, the creeks, the buffalo. His heart ached for The People he had left behind, and—in this dark place that smelled of salt and where strange trees grew beyond the high stone walls, where the water crashed but did not flow, and stretched on farther than any river, any pond, anything Nocona had ever seen—he wondered how long he could remember what home looked like.

One morning, soldier-chief Pratt had his bluecoats pass out paper books to prisoners. Most of The People declined to use these "ledger books," as the bluecoats called them. Ink, crayons, pencils, and some type of paint called "watercolor" came, too. Through sign language, Nocona learned that if he filled one book with drawings, he might be able to sell it to some woman or man from Saint Augustine for two dollars.

White man's money did not appeal to Nocona, but he remembered how much pleasure drawing and coloring had given him, as a boy, and as a man. Back in his homeland, many warriors would seek his advice when they wanted to remember some famous fight, or buffalo hunt, or how the sun rose along Cache Creek, to decorate their lodges, or record some great event on a hide.

He recalled what colors meant to The People. Black for victory or strength, blue for wisdom or confidence, green for harmony or endurance, white for purity or mourning, red for beauty or blood. He remembered what he had to find to create these colors: clays, roots or berries, even those disgusting beets, for red. Limestone, gypsum, seashells he had traded with a Comanchero, for white. Flowers and moss, or algae, for green. Charcoal mixed with animal fat for black. Duck dung for blue. Flowers and buffalo guts for yellow. Yet, here, thanks to the

white men, he could use their crayons, their paints. So Nocona
tried to remember.

He filled the first ledger book, and, indeed, a black robe visiting from some white-man town far to the south paid Nocona
two silver coins for it. The man was a fool. Nocona did not care
much for any of those sketches. They looked like something a
Caddo might have drawn. But he worked again, and finished
another book. By then, he had a helper, a Mexican captive who
had become one of The People. His name was Tana—which
meant *knee*—for his right kneecap had been shattered during a
raid against the Texans, and no longer could it bend. Tana
helped Nocona remember, and Nocona took his time.

When he closed his eyes, Nocona saw the wildflowers, yellow
and orange, that rose above the green grass. He saw the rocks,
reddish or gray and sometimes black, and the cedars and oaks
that twisted this way and that, and beyond those hills, the
granite mountains—the ones the white men called the Wichi-
tas—the clouds, white and gray with the promise of rain, and
the blue skies beyond those clouds that suggested a fine day. He
remembered the river otters, the burrowing owls, the deer, the
turkey, and, yes, the buffalo.

He also knew the *puha*—the power—of those mountains. For
it had been his father's father's second wife's mother's mother
who had used her *puha* to form those mountains, an act that
had saved The People.

While the men were out of camp, hunting buffalo, a runner
dashed across the flats and warned the women, the children,
and the old men that Pawnees were coming, to kill, and scalp,
and destroy. Too many for women and children and old men to
fight, so The People had fled. Yet Nocona's father's father's
second wife's mother's mother remained behind, to pray, to mix
the dirt with an elk horn, and cut her fingers with a knife and
let the blood drip onto the dirt. Then she ran to catch up with

The People and chided them for running. When The People looked back, they saw the mountains that Nocona's father's father's second wife's mother's mother had created. The Pawnees would have to go around these mountains, and by that time, the warriors of The People had returned.

For one moon, Nocona worked on this drawing. He drew the buffalo, and the lodges, and the sun rising just at daybreak. He drew his two wives, his oldest son, and the daughter who had lived only two days before crossing to the other world. He used the "watercolor" paint, but did not mix this with water. Water was plentiful at this salty region, and Nocona knew the kind of *puha* he needed. He used his tears, and the tears from Tana.

In a place like Fort Marion, tears came easily.

At length, the bluecoat with three stripes on his sleeves came to see if Nocona had a ledger to sell to a "society of petticoats"—whatever that meant—visiting the fort. Nocona nodded, but he ripped out this one sketch, the one he and Tana had spent so much time creating. He showed it to the bluecoat.

"That's real good," Three Stripes said, but the words were foreign to Nocona, no matter how much time he spent in one of the rooms listening to a bluecoat try to teach those "wards" the true language called English.

Nocona held the painting against the wall.

"You want to hang it?" Three Stripes asked.

They could not understand each other, but Tana reached back to those years before he became one of The People. He spoke, gutturally, uncertain, and Three Stripes pulled on his chin whiskers.

"That's Mex, ain't it?"

That was a language some white men understood, especially in this Florida, so Three Stripes left and returned with soldier-chief Pratt and another bluecoat. First, they admired the sketch.

It was unlike any the bluecoats had seen. Not even the Cheyennes could do something this . . . this . . . realistic.

"It needs a name," Pratt said. "It'll sell better with a name. And if he signs it."

"He won't sign nothin'," Three Stripes said, not admonishing though, not chiding, merely stating an undisputed fact.

Yes they agreed and they remembered: Nocona was a bloodthirsty savage, an unrepentant heathen, and a malevolent fiend.

"But," Three Stripes said, "the son of a bitch can paint."

"Comanche Camp at Dawn," Pratt said, and Three Stripes and the bluecoat with no stripes knew not to argue with their soldier-chief.

Using his old tongue, Tana told the bluecoats of Nocona's idea, and No Stripes told Three Stripes and soldier-chief Pratt, "He wants to paint this thing on the rocks here, Lieutenant."

Walking to the wall, cold and hard and far from a fitting canvas, Pratt touched the stones. He shook his head, sighing, but when he turned back to Nocona, his eyes locked on the sketch from the ledger.

"I guess," Pratt said, "this place could use some color. See he gets some brushes, Sergeant. For now. Watercolors won't work. Not on this. Buy him some oils." He studied the drawing again. *"Comanche Camp at Dawn."*

"It's better than the stick figures and petroglyphs most of these bucks scratch onto this coquina," No Stripes said.

When the new paints arrived, Nocona and Tana resumed an even harder task. Drawing and coloring on paper was easy, but this shell rock called coquina proved uncompromising. And he still had to fill ledgers to sell to the whites from Saint Augustine. Ledger art took time away from his dream, his wall, but it kept the soldier-chief happy, thinking that, maybe, Nocona was learning to become a white man.

It rained, and the walls leaked water, washing away part of what Nocona had painted that morning, destroying the wildflowers and grass and even Nocona's daughter. He did not need to mix tears with oil paints, but he knew he had to.

Soon, white men and women, touring the fort, newspaper reporters, senators and preachers and drummers would be brought to Nocona's cell, where they would admire this "rock art," and Tana would sell Nocona's ledgers filled with sketches, as well as his own crude drawings.

"Catlin," one woman might say.

"Courbet," a man with a twisted mustache once whispered.

Bodmer.

Renoir.

Moran.

The names were as foreign to Nocona as was this Fort Marion, the strange trees, the white birds, the sweat and the salt and the smells. All that remained real to him was this wall, his work, his memories.

The money always went to paints—for soldier-chief Pratt had started to complain that only one Comanche was doing ledger art, but spending more time on a wall painting, while many Kiowas, Arapahos, and Cheyennes kept producing ledgers. Yet when Nocona realized that he could not afford the paints sold in Saint Augustine—and that clays, beets, and buffalo guts were hard to find on the sandy Atlantic Coast to create paints— Three Stripes shrugged.

"I'll get 'em for you. You can pay me next time."

It took many seasons, maybe longer, of retouching, of reworking, of wiping away water during the storms. Of remembering. Of crying. He had the river otter, and the buffalo, and his family and his friends. He had horses, stolen from those damned Texans, and even his father's father's second wife's mother's mother as he imagined her.

Then Tana tapped himself on his chest, and pointed to a place near the stream where the boys were playing when they were supposed to be watering the horses.

Nocona smiled. He understood. Always, he sketched first, not just to sell to some tourist or dignitary or bluecoat, but so he could get it right on paper. Paper, and watercolors, forgave. Coquina and oil paints did not.

When he drew that right leg straight, unable to bend, Tana choked out a sob. Turning, Nocona stared at this Mexican who had become one of The People, and felt his heart sink. He quickly ripped the paper from the ledger, crumpled it into a ball, and tossed it to the cold, hard floor. The next sketch made Tana whole, able to run, and this was the boy that Nocona spent three days transferring to *Comanche Camp at Dawn*.

Tana did not return to see the painting, but Nocona knew he must hurry. Some strong storm approached, the air filled with a foreboding, a dread. Skies had darkened, and the bluecoats ran around, shouting, screaming, securing boxes and wagons with thick, twisting ropes.

A rainstorm—or this thing the white men feared called a hurricane—would destroy his painting, which, in turn, would kill Nocona. He had to finish. He had to paint himself.

He had no time to sketch first, not the way the wind roared, not the way the bluecoats acted. He did not even know if he had enough paint to finish, but he drew the outline of himself near his lodge, near his two wives. He painted himself looking down at the baby, his daughter, that his second wife held—the daughter he had never seen in her previous life for Nocona had been hunting buffalo near the Palo Duro when she had been

68

born, and when she had died.

He had no mirror, but what good would a reflecting glass do? How did he look now, after all this time in damp, humid Florida? His hair short, wearing a blue coat and white man's leggings. He let tears wet his brush, and began applying the strokes.

At last, Nocona stepped away. Tears made seeing difficult, as did the lack of sun, the dark clouds that covered the sky.

Comanche Camp at Dawn.

It was as it had been, and should be. His heart no longer felt heavy, and what he saw looked . . . almost too real . . . even if only paints and dyes and tears applied to a stone fort's wall. But his *puha* remained strong. He imagined himself stepping into the painting and becoming part of it, forever. Just close his eyes, Nocona told himself, and he would disappear from his world and find himself in The People's camp at dawn.

The tropical storm blew through quickly, and most of the strongest wind, waves, and rain missed Saint Augustine and Fort Marion. Oh, palm trees were uprooted, roofs damaged, and the drawbridge over the fort's moat took three days to repair. Bluecoats joined Cheyennes, Comanches, Kiowas, Arapahos, and Caddos in sweeping rainwater and saltwater out of the cells. One soldier drowned. Another broke his leg. One Arapaho died, a heart attack the post surgeon determined, but he was old anyway and would have died in a week or so. Two Comanches were missing.

Concerning the latter, Lieutenant Pratt kept his report brief. During the storm, most likely, Comanche prisoners Nocona and Tana likely moved to the upper walls, and were either blown off, or jumped down to be battered by the waves and washed into Matanzas Bay. The hostiles were presumed drowned.

Pratt's report struck Sergeant Jeremiah Burgess—Three

Stripes, to Indian prisoners—odd. Why would Nocona and Tana have fled a cell, one of the few cells that had not been flooded during the storm? The painting on the wall remained perfect, and it would stay unblemished for another year until The People and other prisoners were shipped back to their homelands, or to the Indian boarding school in Carlisle, Pennsylvania, or elsewhere.

Yet on that night in October 1877, when that tropical storm damaged but did not destroy Fort Marion, more than twelve hundred miles away in Indian Territory, several Comanches were reported missing from the federal reserve near Fort Sill. A violent twister had blown in that evening, and, well, Comanches had this way of disappearing. Not wanting any extra paperwork, or answering to Washington City, the post commander and the Indian agent decided that those Indians, including the two wives and sons of one of the belligerents sent to Florida, had simply died.

Sergeant Jeremiah Burgess never learned that, of course, but he had his own suspicions of what had happened during that night at Fort Marion. He would often step into the cell that had once housed Nocona, and he would look at the painting on the wall, the one Lieutenant Pratt had named *Comanche Camp at Dawn.*

Hard to believe a Comanche had done that work of art. Up until the time came that Burgess had to bring in two soldiers to whitewash the wall—before some Apache prisoners entered Fort Marion—Burgess would stare at what he considered a masterpiece on coquina.

Sometimes, he swore, the image changed. The boys playing in the creek with the horses appeared to move. The Comanche staring at the little tyke in the mother's arms might even seem to grin at Burgess. Once, after payday, he entered the cell near midnight and thought that *Comanche Camp at Dawn* had turned into a Comanche camp at night. But that had to be the shadows from his candle, not to mention the whiskey. Another time, he almost swore he could smell woodsmoke, and see it snaking through the openings in the Comanche teepees.

Crazy, but Burgess knew in his heart that those two Comanches had not been swept into the bay in October of '77. They had simply painted themselves into this painting. It looked so damned real, Burgess dreamed that he could just step into the painting.

Applying the whitewash, the private from Rhode Island shook his head, and commented, not really to the other soldier or Sergeant Burgess: "Hard to believe some redskin done this."

"What'd you say his name was, Sarge?" asked the other soldier.

"Nocona," Three Stripes answered.

"He was a bloodthirsty savage, an unrepentant heathen, and a malevolent fiend—but the son of a bitch could paint."

Plantin' Season

Far as we could tell, the two dead men had nothin' in common, not at first, nohow. Strangers they was, to us and themselves, when they sat down inside Jess Leach's bucket of blood and commenced playin' poker. If they introduced themselves, Jess never heard 'em, and he didn't ask nothin' hisself because Jess is a polite sort of fellow. So forty minutes and too much forty-rod later, them two strangers pulled out their six-shooters and blasted one another to kingdom come.

Now, truth be told, things like that happened with some frequency on Willow Creek each spring, when folks started comin' back to the mountains to work their claims. Most miners and townsfolk knowed better than to winter in this country, no sir. They'd head south, spend their earnin's, then come back when the snow began meltin' to make their piles again. You see, miners, and the parasites that follow 'em, tend to be like rattlers. When they come out of hibernation, their tempers are short-fused and hard.

Jess called it Plantin' Season, and, come every spring, we planted many a man up on the ridge overlookin' our town of canvas tents and rawhide log affairs like Jess Leach's saloon.

The spring I tell about, however, proved to be a mite different only 'cause, like I done said, Jess Leach is a polite fellow, and a man of his word, unlike most beer-jerkers who work gold towns. Which brings me to the two dead strangers at Jess's Mayflower Saloon. The shootin' didn't last long. Seldom do.

72

The fellow with the handlebar mustache, he expired immediately, but the other gent, the one in the black broadcloth and high-topped boots with pretty crescent moon inlays, he lasted a few moments, chokin' on his blood and the thick white smoke that clouded the insides of Jess's place the way it always done durin' Plantin' Season.

"I'm kilt," the man told Jess. "Don't bury me in some unknown grave."

Problem was, he joined the fellow with that well-groomed mustache before he could tell Jess exactly what his name was, so there they lay amongst the sawdust and blood, with Jess just a-squattin' there and scratchin' his beard when I come upon the scene after hearin' the shots and enterin' the Mayflower to investigate.

First thing I done was hold a coroner's inquest, not that we had a coroner or nothin', but we was tryin' to be as legal as we could in the Territory. I brung in six good citizens for my jury, had Doc Towner examine the two dead men, which we placed up on Jess's two billiard tables—shipped all the way from St. Louis by way of Santa Fe—and then got down to business.

The only witness to the shootin' in question was Jess, and he told Doc, me, and the jury that he really hadn't seen nothin', busy as he was behind the bar waterin' down the latest batch of whiskey, when he heard the first gunshot. Then a misfire. Then several more shots. When the ruction ceased, he took a cautious peek over the top of his bar and seen that the two men had shot each other down.

Next, Doc Towner identified the two pistols found on the floor, a Starr revolver with four shots fired and one failed percussion cap, and a Navy Colt with two rounds spent. The Starr allegedly belonged to the man with the fancy mustache, and, accordin' to Doc's testimony, rounds had struck the gent with the nice boots twice in the chest while another ball must

73

have taken off the man's left index finger. That victim had placed two rounds in the throat of the man sportin' the tonsorial masterpiece.

"Some shootin'," Clay Bakker, one of my jurors, commented.

"Scratch shot," Ben Tiedeman argued.

"Have you ever seen either of the men in question?" I asked.

"No," Jess said. "Don't recognize 'em from last fall or nothin'. They was strangers."

"How about you, Doc?"

"Can't say I've seen either man before. Probably both of them came in to set up a game."

I told Doc I couldn't allow such testimony as it was speculation, and instructed the jurors to ignore what Doc Towner had just said.

"I never listen to that old goat nohow," Ben Tiedeman commented, and I had to threaten Ben with contempt of court before askin' Ben and Clay and Zeke Newton, Baz Salazar, Mountain Gallagher, and Placer Bill, my jurors, to file by Jess's billiard tables and see if they had ever seen either of the late arrivals to Willow Creek.

None of 'em had.

Thus I made my rulin', which I would send on down to the Capital, that on Tuesday the 13th inst., two men, unknown in these parts, rode into the Willow Creek minin' camp and entered the Mayflower Saloon at approximately the same time, and approximately forty minutes after their arrival, for reasons unknown, with pistols then and there loaded and charged with gunpowder and leaden balls did then and there put said pistols in their hands and then and there unlawfully feloniously and of their malice aforethought did shoot off and discharge at one another into their own bodies aforesaid leaden balls out of aforesaid revolvers by force of the aforesaid gunpowder and fall onto the floor of the aforesaid Mayflower Saloon, owned by Mr.

Jess Leach, in the aforesaid settlement on Willow Creek in this Territory, and thusly then and there expire of mortal wounds inflicted upon themselves.

"That's all settled," I said, and asked Jess to pour us all a drink that we would bill to the Capital. We'd plant the two boys, and also invoice the Capital for our services, divide up their money and wares, and be done with the matter.

"Well, there's one other thing." Jess went and told me about the fellow with the fancy boots and his wish to have his handle on his marker.

"He didn't tell you his name?" I asked.

"No. He just died."

Now, me, I was a mite thirsty, but Placer Bill began claimin' that a man should be remembered and it really weren't fittin' to have some crooked cross over one for all of eternity without a name or nothin' on it to remember him by. And I told Placer Bill that it really didn't matter because if he rode up to the cemetery, he would be hard-pressed to find the names of anyone that we planted last Plantin' Season 'cause winters and the like is hard on graves.

Which worked Zeke Newton into a snit 'cause he had burnt the names of the dead, at least the names we knowed, onto the crosses and pine plank markers with his runnin' iron. "If somebody wants to be remembered, let him buy hisself a marble monument and have it shipped up from Santa Fe," Zeke said.

"No one's blamin' you, Zeke," I said, and told my herd to get itself in line, that all we had to do was learn the name of the man with the handsome mustache.

"No," Jess said, "he didn't say nothin'. It was this fellow here who wanted to be remembered."

Thusly, I began to go through the man's broadcloth coat, but while I was findin' not much of nothin' except a box of lucifers, pipe tobacco, and L.I. Cohen playin' cards, Baz Salazar said we should not forget the man with the mustache, neither, that he had a right to be remembered at least till next Plantin' Season. I muttered an oath, my throat awful parched, but Doc Towner agreed and then and there searched for some identification on the other expired stranger.

Still, all Doc turned up was a Barlow knife, plug tobacco, and yet another box of L.I. Cohen cards.

"See," Doc said all haughtily. "I told you they were both here to gamble. Why else would they have extra decks of cards?"

Well, I was some frustrated because I recollected that durin' the Plantin' Season of '70, we come across a stranger who got caught in a flash flood but at least he had a letter that had been posted to him from his sister in Bowlin' Green, Kentucky, as the writin' on the letter wasn't too washed out and faded, so we knowed his name even if Zeke Newton didn't burn it on his cross with a runnin' iron as the drowned man had not made no such dyin' request.

Upon Clay Bakker's suggestion—"Let's check their horses!"—we all piled outside. One horse was a bay gelding, the other a buckskin mare, but we turned up no form of names, even when we unsaddled the two mounts and looked to see if perchance a name might have been carved on the underside of their saddles.

Nothin'.

By jacks, the horses didn't even carry brands none of us had ever recognized before.

"Well," I said. "Let's have ourselves a whiskey and think on this matter."

Thusly, at last, I slaked my thirst, and we leaned against the bar and studied on our predicament.

"Maybe we should call one man Mister Starr and the other man Mister Navy," Ben Tiedeman allowed as he fingered the revolvers that had belonged to the recently deceased strangers in question.

"No," Jess said. "That ain't right."

"I wonder," Baz Salazar said, "how come they killed each other."

"Maybe it was over a woman," said Mountain Gallagher.

"Maybe one was on the dodge," Zeke Newton guessed.

"No, then how come they would sit down to play poker together if one was a-chasin' tuther?" said Clay Bakker.

"Who plays two-handed poker anyhow?" asked Placer Bill.

"Gamblers!" Doc Towner shouted. "I tell you they were gamblers."

About that time I finally noticed that durin' all that shootin', the table where they was playin' that final game of cards had remained undisturbed. One chair had been overturned, and Clay Bakker had borrowed the other so he could sit down while he was servin' on my jury, but even the money remained in the pot, exceptin' the gold piece I had procured while nobody was lookin'.

Curious, I ambled over to that table again, and looked at the deck, the top card, a jack of diamonds, splattered with blood. I counted and examined the money in the pot, yellowbacks and greenbacks and some coin, but nothin' that could identify either Fancy Boots or Fancy Mustache. And then I studied the cards, the hand each man held at the time of his demise.

Suddenly, I laughed, and announced I had learnt the names of both men and we could proceed with the plantin' at the cemetery atop the ridge. Everyone got all excited, except Zeke Newton, who frowned when I told him I had no need of his runnin' iron for this plantin'. Instead, I fetched tacks and a ball-peen hammer from the shed next to Jess's waterin' hole as we hauled off the two men to their final restin' place.

Not only that, I now knowed why they had shot each other so I could change my official report, even if I wasn't quite sure which stranger had really been the cause of it all. Mayhap both of 'em.

Jess Leach, he got all upset upon learnin' what I was up to, but I told him I was the closest thing to a judge and there wasn't much point to argue on the matter no longer as Fancy Boots and Fancy Mustache would get ripe if we kept dickerin' over picayune matters.

Baz Salazar nailed a couple of crosses while Clay Bakker, Ben Tiedeman, Placer Bill, and Mountain Gallagher dug the graves. We wrapped Fancy Mustache in his sugans and tossed him into the pit, and covered Fancy Boots in his saddle blanket and dropped him next door.

Doc Towner thought I was right on the mark, but Jess Leach said I wasn't so blasted funny. On Fancy Boots's cross, I took out hammer and tacks and fastened to his grave marker his poker hand:

> Ace of hearts
> Ace of clubs
> Ace of spades
> King of clubs
> King of diamonds

On Fancy Mustache's grave, I nailed up:

> Ace of clubs
> Ace of spades
> Ace of diamonds
> King of spades
> King of hearts

Jess didn't speak to me for a month, but then he accepted how I had fulfilled the dyin' stranger's request as best we could.

Fancy Boots was remembered, and so, for that matter, was Fancy Mustache. By grab, folks at Willow Creek come up to the cemetery just to look at them two graves and laugh at how they both most likely was cheatin' at cards and killed each other. For certain-sure, them two was the tourist attraction that Plantin' Season, I mean to tell you.

Naturally, it didn't last. A raven must have made off with Fancy Mustache's ace of spades, and a late blue norther blowed in come May and took down every single king except Fancy Boots's diamond. In mid-October, I headed south, and by the time I rode back north next April, not only had all the cards disappeared, but so had the crosses Baz Salazar had fixed—just like I had done told Placer Bill—blowed down by the wind and washed away with the snowmelt, I reckon.

That made Jess Leach a mite sad, but he cheered up real soon because it was Plantin' Season again, and that was the year we lynched Ben Tiedeman, and ol' Ben's tombstone became the popular tourist attraction in Willow Creek as Zeke Newton had burned on that piece of warped pine with his runnin' iron.

Here Lies

Ben Tiedeman

Hanged By Mistake

Some kid, we think it was Little Jimmy Roripaugh, later wrote underneath that, "The joke's on us."

Jess Leach didn't find that funny, neither, but he's gettin' over it this Plantin' Season, which is when I take pencil in hand in the Mayflower Saloon to record these recollections.

You see, I reckon this'll be the last Plantin' Season at Willow Creek 'cause the claims have all played out and there ain't hardly a body comin' here this year, exceptin' cowmen, while most miners and merchants be optin' for the diggin's up in

Summit County. Won't nobody remember the two card cheaters, not even Ben Tiedeman, a few months from now, but we'll have ourselves one more fine Plantin' Season the way I hear some cowmen talk inside Jess Leach's bucket of blood.

If I was a bettin' man, I'd lay good money down that we'll be plantin' Zeke Newton 'fore long. That fellow is a mite too handy with a runnin' iron.

Umpire Colt

It happened, Mama said, like this:

On a Sunday afternoon, two years before I was born—"the most beautiful day I've ever seen," Mama called it—Papa took her to a baseball game pitting the Kansas City Antelopes against their biggest rivals, the Pomeroys from Atchison, Kansas.

"The sky a perfect blue," Mama recalled with this dreamy look in her green eyes, "a cool breeze blowing, a lovely afternoon, and everyone in the stadium on their best behavior."

To which Papa grunted, shook his head, and said, "Wasn't no stadium. They played that game in a couple of vacant lots near Fourteenth and Oak. Place stank like wet chicken dung. Best behavior? A bunch of b'hoys, most of them from Atchison, but quite a few local rogues, players and spectators, all in their cups. You and me was the only sober folks there, Mama. And a lovely day? Criminy, it was hotter than the hinges of Hell."

Mama ignored him—she was good at that, although I could tell how Papa's interruption annoyed her. Still, she took a deep breath, let it out so wistfully, and smiled, reaching over to brush the bangs out of my eyes.

"And then he showed up."

He was Wild Bill Hickok.

"Six-foot-three and then some, wearing striped trousers tucked inside these fine boots, blacker than midnight, curly auburn hair hanging past the collar of his Prince Albert, and the breeze carried the scent of those long, lovely, perfumed

81

locks all the way to where I sat. He walked so gracefully, and he picked up the baseball with his left hand, and, with long, tapered fingers, tossed the ball to the hurler. Fingers made to play a Mozart concerto on a Steinway Square Grand at the Opera Hall."

Papa chuckled. "Fingers made for them two Navy Colts he had tucked in his sash."

Ignoring yet another interruption, Mama continued: "He pushed back a wide-brimmed hat, and said, 'Play.' "

Papa shook his head. "Mama, you done left out that the reason Wild Bill took to umpiring that game was on account a riot broke out—hard rocks from Atchison was always causing a ruction—and the beer-jerker who had been umpiring the game run toward the Blue River for his life."

"He was magnificent," Mama continued, meaning Wild Bill, not Papa or the fleeing beer-jerker.

"Well," Papa agreed, "nobody argued over nary a call Wild Bill made, that's certain-sure. But he sure made some horrible ones. Man's vision must've already been fading after some two-bit chirpy give him that disease."

"Hush!" Some things Mama would not tolerate, or pretend she hadn't heard.

Papa's lips flattened, and he crossed his arms, straightened in the silk-tapestry Napoleon chair so abruptly the legs scraped the wooden floor and caused my skin to crawl. He let Mama begin her story.

"It was August 12, 1866, a beautiful Sunday," Mama said, "and citizens flocked to the stadium after church to watch the deciding game between our Antelopes and the Pomeroys."

"Most was coming straight from the saloons, dance halls, and cribs," Papa whispered conspiratorially to me. "The only ones coming from church was them Methodists who was having a cow that the city would allow a sporting game to be played on the Sabbath."

Well, the game had originally been scheduled for Saturday, but had been postponed because of rain.

"Which made that afternoon so un-tolerable muggy," Papa said.

Atchison had won the first contest, Kansas City the second, making this the game for the bragging rights.

With the War of the Rebellion over—unless you counted those gangs of unreconstructed bushwhackers still roaming across Missouri—Kansas City boomed from a city of 4,500 before the War to a thriving metropolis of perhaps 15,000. Many of them were only temporary residents, bound West, migrating from the East, the North, across the Atlantic, and the war-ravaged South, bringing with them all sorts of wonders that this not-long-ago frontier hamlet had never seen.

Including baseball.

"Now," Papa explained while Mama poured tea, "I had seen a couple of those games back at Jefferson Barracks. Taken a fancy to it, so after me and your mama got hitched, and I'd heard some of the boys at the packing plant saying how fine them games between the Pomeroys and Antelopes had been, and since I had Sunday off, of course, I asked her if she'd care to come along and see this fine sport."

Mama reached over to pat Papa's hand. "It was the best question you ever asked me," she said, "and I'm so happy that I said yes."

Which left Papa looking as if he'd just given up a game-winning home run to Sliding Billy Hamilton.

"Well, those vile first nine of the Pomeroys had trounced us savagely when we played in Atchison," Mama said, though this had to be all secondhand since she had never even crossed the Kansas line, "but that was because of the biased umpires. And when we routed them in Kansas City, they complained that—

dare not you believe it, son—our honest umpire made egregious calls."

"We whupped the tar out of them," Papa said as Mama slid a cup and saucer toward him, another toward me, and picked up her own to sip.

"So on that afternoon," Mama said a moment later, "when our valiant Antelopes jumped out to a twenty-to-five lead after two innings, well, anyone who dare lives in Atchison lacks class. Yes, lacks any class, at all."

I tried to picture in my mind just what a "valiant antelope" would look like, and Papa said, "That started the riot."

"A disagreement," Mama corrected.

Said Papa: "A disagreement that sent six spectators to their pill-rollers, landed a Pomeroy hurler in the hospital, and left Bobby Byrne with a raw slab of meat over his right eye during much of that day's game and for two nights after that."

And the umpire, I remembered, running for his life toward the Blue River.

According to Mama, when some semblance of order had been restored, the manager of the Antelopes stormed to the pitcher's box and cried out, "Well, now what? We cannot play without an umpire!"

To which the Pomeroys manager/first baseman said, "We could not play with the last one!"

The Antelopes' leader pointed at the stands and said, "There's Thomas Speers, a man known far and wide for his honesty."

"Tom Speers," Papa let me know, "was Kansas City's—the Missouri side, of course—chief of police."

Which caused me to set down my teacup: "Wait a minute. The police chief was at the game?"

"Sure," Papa said, "and about half the department. We was playing Atchison."

"And no one tried to stop the riot?" I asked.

"Disagreement," Mama corrected.

"It run its course right quick," Papa said. "A few busted heads. Only real bad injury was when Ace Grace laid out that Pomeroy hurler with his bat-stick." Papa sniggered at the memory. "Cracked his skull, certain-sure, and if Ace could have hit a ball like that, he would've been on the first nine and not just some muffin."

Then, Mama cleared her throat and told us: "Chief Speers, of course, declined, saying it would not be proper for him to umpire a baseball game as two policemen played for the Antelopes."

Which is when someone shouted, "How 'bout him?"

Him, of course, was Wild Bill Hickok, sitting under a parasol, wiping beer suds off his handsome mustache. The crowd began chanting, "Wild Bill! Wild Bill! Wild Bill!" Louder, Mama recalled, than any of the cheers for Pomeroys or Antelopes, which must have irritated Ace Grace and all the other athletes.

Finally, Wild Bill rose, tipped his hat to some ladies, and stepped into the sun and onto the field.

"Can he be fair?" someone asked.

"Boys," Wild Bill said, removing his hat, "I am a deputy United States marshal. Born in Illinois. Come here by way of Nebraska and Springfield. I am not one of the local men. I got friends in Atchison, just like I got friends here."

The hat returned to his head, and his right hand resumed its place on the grip of one of his Navy Colts.

"You got no call to wonder," he concluded.

"But do you know the rules?" a Pomeroy called out.

"I like this game," he answered. "Seen it played some during the War. Bring me a rule book."

Well, the only copy anyone had was *Beadle's Dime Base-Ball Player: A Compendium of the Game* by Henry Chadwick. It was the 1860 version, six years out of date, but the managers of both teams pointed out some of the important changes over the past six years.

Mainly, from the meeting at Clinton Hall back in December of '64, that the ball had to be caught in the air—and not also on the first bound—to be ruled an out. And, of course, from 1863, that if a pitcher deliberately did not throw the striker fair balls, the umpire could warn him first, and then call balls. Three balls, and the striker would be awarded first base.

"And there ain't no soaking!" cried out the Antelopes' manager, Big Boy Evans.

"Like hell," said Murdering Jim Watson.

"What's 'soaking'?" Wild Bill asked.

Which, Mama told me, was when a player in the field threw the ball at the base runner, and if the ball hit the runner before the runner reached base, that runner was out. Often, the runner was out, literally, until he could be revived or hauled to a doctor.

"Kind of like buffaloing a drunk with the barrel of my Navy." Wild Bill grinned. "I like that rule. It's in." He fetched a pencil from the inside pocket of his Prince Albert and scribbled it in the *Compendium*. "Soaking is allowed," he said aloud as he penciled in the words.

"But that's been banned since '45," Big Boy complained.

"Like hell," Murdering Jim Watson said.

"It's in." Wild Bill returned pencil to pocket and hand to a Navy's butt.

Crazy Curtis Spivey, the Pomeroys' loudest blowhard, spit out a river of tobacco juice, wiped his lips, swollen a mite after that go at fisticuffs during the previous disagreement, shifted the bat-stick in his hand, and said: "Rule book says that the umpire's gotta be familiar with every single point of the game. He ain't."

The crowd went silent. Murdering Jim Watson and Big Boy Evans took a few steps away from home plate. Most of the Pomeroys who had been standing near the blowhard decided to slake their thirsts from the keg of beer near their bench.

"But Wild Bill," Mama remembered, "just kept on reading. Didn't look up. He was so deft, so agile, he could read that book with one hand, letting the breeze turn the page whenever need be."

"Keeping that other hand on a Navy," Papa reminded me.

When the book finally closed, Wild Bill faced the braggart.

"Rule book I got says that the umpire must be 'manly,' 'fearless,' and 'impartial.' You implying I ain't?"

Spivey's face turned ashen, and Wild Bill walked over to him, and held the rule book out. "Take it," he ordered, and the blowhard did. "Hold it just like that," Wild Bill said, and Spivey obeyed, holding the book in his trembling left hand about head high. Wild Bill walked back toward the pitcher's box, forty-five feet from the plate, and the blowhard was standing fifteen feet beyond that. When Wild Bill reached the box, he turned, drew one of the Colts from his sash, and two shots sounded like one.

"He put two holes right through that emblem of a dime on the cover of that book," Mama said. "So graceful, so gallant."

"And Spivey put something in his own britches." Papa slapped his thigh. "Had to walk out of the park, to hoots and howls of Antelopes, spectators, and a few of his own Pomeroys."

Wild Bill's eyesight, I guess, wasn't so bad after all.

Players took their positions, and the crowd settled in to watch the game.

"It was a beautiful ballpark," Mama said, "even lovelier than 'The Hole.' " Which is where Kansas City's team plays these days.

In accordance with the rules, the pitcher's box was a six-foot square, home plate a twelve-inch square, and second base a nine-inch "fixed iron circular plate."

"Home plate," Papa told me, "was the cover off a book somebody had stole from St. Louis Mercantile Library, and second base was a circular blade from a sawmill east of town. Whitewashed, of course, but the flecks of rust was showing more than the whitewash by August."

So Wild Bill slid that bullet-riddled *Compendium* inside his sash, took a spot slightly behind and to the right of the pitcher's box, and the first Pomeroys striker stepped to the plate.

Thus resumed the deciding game between the Antelopes, in their knickers and blue-striped ball caps, and the Pomeroys, in their green shield-front shirts and flat-crowned straw hats.

He made it through two innings—only two base runners got soaked, much to Wild Bill's disappointment—but that day proved to be a scorcher, so between the fourth and fifth innings, Wild Bill removed his Prince Albert, folded it gently, searched the stands, and approached a certain lovely lady sitting near the first-base bench.

"Ma'am," he said, "I'd be honored if you would keep my coat." When she accepted, he bowed and handed her the Prince Albert.

Mama's eyes brightened at the memory. She had to stop, almost out of breath, as if it were 1866 again and she were folding Wild Bill Hickok's coat across her lap.

"He had such gentle eyes," Mama said.

"And dandruff," Papa said, "but Mama done a right smart job brushing it off that coat."

Before returning to the playing field, Wild Bill took a sip from a canteen—water, if you believed Mama; rye, if Papa had the story right—and then walked to his spot on the field. Murdering Jim Watson grabbed his bat-stick and waited for Wild Bill to call "play."

"Only . . ." Mama had to stop. She shivered.

Even Papa leaned forward as if hearing the story for the first time.

I held my breath, waiting. Mama spoke, her voice a whisper, "He did not call 'play,' for the next words we heard were . . ." Her voice rose to such a shout, I almost fell over backwards in my chair.

"Wild Bill Hickok, I'll kill you darned son of a cur!"

"Pardon my language," Mama told me, her voice normal once more, "but that's what that heathen said."

"Actually," Papa said, "he said—"

"Hush."

Papa hushed.

Across the vacant lot that served as center field strode Crazy Curtis Spivey, who had changed into clean duck trousers, and no longer carried a bat-stick but a .44-caliber Colt's Dragoon revolver.

"Bobby Byrne was hurling for us," Mama said, "despite his black eye suffered during the prior disagreement, and when Bobby saw Crazy Curtis Spivey making a beeline across center field, he rushed past Wild Bill and fled to the Antelopes' bench."

Papa nodded. "Almost knocked Wild Bill on his fanny."

Spivey's first shot spanged off the saw blade that served as second base. Which sent all of the players and plenty of those observing the game well out of the path of any wild shots.

Children cried.

Dogs barked.

Women muttered prayers.

Men spit out tobacco juice.

Chief of Police Thomas Speers gaped.

Wild Bill slowly strode inside the pitcher's box, and let Crazy Curtis Spivey keep on approaching.

"The second shot hit John Spielman's Studebaker," Mama said.

"Missed Hickok by a mile," Papa said. "Served Spielman, that sorry skinflint, right for parking that close to the field."

"Served him right for having the audacity to cheer for the Pomeroys when he lived in Kansas City," Mama said.

"But he lived on the Kansas side," Papa said.

"No matter."

Spivey fired again, and this shot clipped some of the tassels on Wild Bill's sash. The crazed man with clean pants kept walking. And Wild Bill?

"He stood there, calm, as if he were watching a mother take her toddler for a stroll in the park," Mama said. "One hand gripped the revolver on his left side, but the other remained behind his back."

When Spivey reached second base, which now had a huge gash in it as a result from his errant shot, he stopped, thumbed back the heavy hammer on the Dragoon, and brought up the revolver deliberately, calmly.

"I'll kill you now," he said.

Silence.

Papa and I waited.

"We never even saw Wild Bill move," Mama said softly. "He was that fast. There was a crack, and a groan, and I closed my eyes. When I looked up, everyone was cheering, those watching the game, John Spielman, Antelopes and even Pomeroys. Everyone there. Except Wild Bill Hickok."

Papa nodded. "And Crazy Curtis Spivey, lying spread-eagle at second base."

More silence.

I cleared my throat. "Wild Bill shot him?"

Mama blinked, stared at me, and said, "At a baseball game? Oh, son, of course not."

"Nailed him," Papa said, "right between his eyes."

"With a baseball," Mama explained. "The one Bobby Byrne

must have dropped into Wild Bill's right hand when he fled the pitcher's box." She sighed, and said, "Poor Wild Bill . . . he would have made a masterful hurler for any baseball club."

"Tom Speers," Papa said, "ordered a couple of his coppers, ones not playing for our Antelopes, to haul Spivey to the calaboose . . ." He chuckled, leaned toward me, and said, "He'd soiled his britches again. Spivey never played again, lessen they let him at the prison yard in Jefferson City."

Mama sighed again. "He was so magnificent."

Meaning Wild Bill, not Curtis Spivey, Papa, or Bobby Byrne.

The clock chimed, and Papa pushed himself up from his chair. "We best be heading to 'The Hole' " he said. "Seats fill up early when the Boston Beaneaters come to town."

He helped Mama out of her seat.

"It was the first, and greatest, baseball game I ever saw," Mama told me. "And afterward, a nickel-plated Columbus phaeton drawn by two of the most beautiful gray Connemara stallions ever born, pulled up behind home plate. And Wild Bill fetched his Prince Albert, kissed my hand, bowed to the crowd, and climbed into the carriage."

By then, Mama had closed her eyes, picturing her gallant hero, and Papa mouthed at me: "With a strumpet hanging on both arms."

"He rode away," Mama whispered, "like a king."

Silence again hung in our parlor as Papa found his hat, and Mama got her parasol, until I found the courage to ask: "Yeah, but who won the game?"

"We did," they answered in unison. "Forty-eight to twenty-eight."

"Those Pomeroys from Atchison never stood no chance playing our Antelopes," Papa said.

"Especially when Wild Bill Hickok was umpiring," Mama said.

And we left home, to watch the Boston Beaneaters play Kansas City in a game that might not have been so one-sided had Wild Bill Hickok been around to umpire that one, too.

THE SAN ANGELA
STUMP MATCH OF 1876

When it was all said and done—after one-and-a-half kegs of lukewarm pilsner and nine bottles of Old Overholt (although Sergeant Searles figured only the first two bottles contained rye, after which the beer-jerker served forty-rod in Old Overholt bottles)—Thelonious Friend blamed it all on the muffin nine from Ben Ficklin.

No, cowhand Luke Sundee argued, that appeared too obvious, and he put Friend at fault because if it hadn't been for that trooper's big mouth, foreman Jake McKendree never would've picked up no bat-stick to begin with. Sundee's pard, Slim Byrne, blamed Luke Sundee. McKendree broke up that fight—but only after he felt sure Byrne had won—and collected his dollar from June Raines.

Using the arm he could still lift, trumpeter Napoleon Trice pointed at Ban Higgins and called him the culprit, whilst First Sergeant George Akins laid it all on McKendree's dealing off the bottom, to which McKendree called Akins an error-prone muffin, and everybody prepared for a go at fisticuffs when Captain R.H.M. Galloway put things in proper perspective.

Being a man of letters—and I don't mean the initials he used for his handle or even because he could actually read—the captain said the one most answerable to what transpired had to be A.G. Spalding, or whoever it was that actually writ the 1876 edition of the *Official Base Ball Guide*.

Which is why, other than the fact that he was an officer in the

11th and them infantry boys tend to be pretty good on their feet, we had elected Cap Galloway to umpire the San Angela Stump Match of 1876, which wasn't played exactly in San Angela but did occur in '76.

" 'Article II,' " Cap read. " 'Objects . . . To encourage, foster, and elevate the game of base ball . . . To enact and enforce proper rules for the exhibition and conduct of the game . . .' But mostly, it is spelled out in the third objective . . ." Here he closed that volume and recited from memory, and he could recollect real good, even when in his cups. " 'To make base ball playing respectable and honorable.' "

To which I said: "I ain't rightly sure we accomplished that, Cap."

This was September, but there wouldn't have been no stump match if the Bar J-5 boys hadn't interrupted a game on the flats along the North Concho River in April.

Napoleon Trice had just requested a low ball be delivered by hurler Mike Searles when Luke Sundee loped down the right-field baseline, raising dust that prompted a cussing fit from Diamond Henry, whose real name was Henry Diamond but had changed the order oncet he discovered base ball, even if, ask me, Henry Diamond sounded just as good.

"The hell are you doin' on our range?" Sundee yelled.

"The hell does it look like?" shortstop Wil Bloford barked.

Ever the peacekeeper, I stepped away from my umpiring duties to explain: "It's base ball, Luke. And this ain't nobody's range."

"Base ball!" Sundee spit. "You want to play that damnyankee game, play it at Fort Concho."

"The officers won't let us use their diamond," Sergeant Akins explained.

"Don't make no nevermind to me." The cowhand jerked his

thumb toward a cloud of dust that he had not raised. "We got forty head comin', and you'll get trampled if you don't move out of our way."

Let me explain: First, Tom Green County covers a lot of country so we wasn't in nobody's way. Next, the 10th was buffalo soldiers, meaning they be ex-slaves wearing Union blue in Texas, whilst the Bar J-5 was white Texans who wore the gray during that late unpleasantness. Last, troopers and cowhands hardly never got along nohow.

Afore Akins and Sundee went to a-tussling, Jake McKendree galloped up. More words got spoke, the gist being base ball was a manly activity that required skill, unlike punching cattle in which the horse done all the work . . . or that the only game of any kind worth a-playing was faro, unless it got dealt by some sharper at Tubby O'Halloran's bucket of blood in Ben Ficklin.

Finally, Thelonious Friend challenged McKendree with: "If you think it's so easy, you try gettin' a hit." Never one to let no challenge go unanswered, McKendree swung down from his sorrel, snatched away Trice's bat-stick, and screamed at Sergeant Searles to throw the damned cow pie, which wasn't no cow pie at all but a bona fide base ball that weighed between the required five and five-and-a-quarter ounces, or had afore Corporal Marcus McTrammick knocked it into the North Concho and saddler Jeremiah Sherman dropped it in the sand after a-muffing Friend's knee-deep throw out of the river.

Well, McKendree missed the first two strikes, but drilled the third past a diving Bloford's outstretched left hand.

"There!" The Bar J-5 ramrod slammed the bat-stick in the dirt. Jeremiah Sherman run in, however, plucked the ball in left-center field afore it rolled into the prickly pear, and throwed to first baseman Jeremiah Sherman.

"The striker," I said, quite pleased with myself, "is out."

"What the hell do you mean?" McKendree shouted.

"You got to reach safely afore the fielder throws to the base," I explained.

"What base?"

I pointed at trooper Wil Bloford's slouch hat.

More arguing commenced—"I hit the ball!" "That don't make it no base hit!" "Cowboys don't run nowheres when they can ride!" "Jeremiah woulda throwed out that bag of bones, too!"—about the rules of the game.

The argument got continued at the War Paint Saloon.

"I don't see why you stick up for them bluecoats and their damnyankee game," Plug Hat Charly told me. "You served under John Bell Hood."

"Because," I let the waddie know, "I spent eighteen months at Rock Island. Learned the game watching Yankee guards play. Later played with the guards. And I get paid Yankee script to scout for them buffalo soldiers, who earn their pay a-protecting you-all from Indians."

"Comanch' ain't no problem for nobody no more," Ray Birmingham reminded me.

"And we," Tubby O'Halloran said, "can lick those Concho boys or any nine the Bar J-5 fields."

"Who the hell," McKendree and I said like we was singing a duet, "brung you into our conversation?"

When he wasn't a-running his gambling den, O'Halloran captained a town-ball team in Ben Ficklin, the dusty county seat five miles down the South Concho River that boasted a subscription school and a stagecoach station but nary a decent ballist among the five hundred fools that lived there. Naturally, neither Fort Concho's officers nor enlisted men deemed O'Halloran's team worthy foes for no base-ball contest, so Ben Ficklin didn't get to play nobody except themselves.

More challenges went this way and tuther afore Cap Galloway scraped chair legs across the floor and sat beside us.

"Why don't you play a stump match?" said Cap, who then explained what a stump match was.

"We play you in a game of base ball?" McKendree contemplated the proposal. "If we win, you walk back to San Angela. If you win, we walk. And the losers stand in the middle of Concho Avenue, singing that the winners are the best ballists in West Texas. That's the bet?"

Cap reminded us of Rule III, Section 2, but everybody agreed—since neither the Bar J-5 nor the 10th Cavalry had been accepted into the newfangled National League of Professional Base Ball Clubs—that the rule banning players from a-betting on games get ignored.

"How about letting us play the winner?" Tubby O'Halloran said.

"When you get a real team, come see us," McKendree said, which caused me to spit rye out my nose. The Bar J-5 didn't have no team, and the only rules McKendree knowed was that you had to beat the throw to the base to be safe and players wasn't supposed to bet on no ball games.

Sergeant Akins wanted me to umpire, but Luke Sundee countered that I wasn't impartial, so everyone, even O'Halloran, voted that handle on Cap Galloway. A date got set for September, after the boys had trailed a herd to Dodge City and after second baseman Jimmy Rose and left fielder Lucius Redman finished their sentences in Fort Concho's stockade. It also give McKendree enough time to buy hisself one of Spalding's rule books, a bat-stick, and a ball for his team.

On the second Sunday in September, we met at the designated field, the "we" being the 10th's first nine and one substitute, Napoleon Trice, if needed, and was; and the Bar J-5 team and a substitute, Ray Birmingham, if needed, who weren't. The field was a diamond we all helped carve out spitting distance from the Middle Concho River, as the 10th refused to play on the South Concho and the cowboys wouldn't compete on the North Concho. No spectators come, this being the Sabbath and most folks in San Angela and at Fort Concho not sobered up from Saturday. Cap Galloway, and his rule book, arrived by surrey. Me, appointed keeper of the scorebook, and everybody else come a-horseback—except some strangers who rid up in a Studebaker.

"McKendree has some new riders," Cap mentioned as I ground-reined my dapple along the river bottoms.

You couldn't help but notice them dudes a-stepping down from that buckboard.

No boots, but baseball shoes. No chaps, neither, but stockings that come up to what Diamond Henry thought was jodhpurs but I allowed was padded base-ball pants. Web belts instead of suspenders. Three had bib-front shirts, like the one Plug Hat Charly wore, but theirs actually had bibs and all the buttons, not to mention fancy letters on the fronts, whilst the other one donned a lace-up shirt. Instead of battered old Bosses of the Plains, fancy pillbox caps topped their noggins.

The colors didn't match. The left fielder and hurler had fancy M's on their white bibs and two black stripes on their caps. A maroon C stood out on the blue bib of the second baseman, whose cap was the color of his C.

"Does Dodge City have a town team?" Sergeant Akins asked.

"Most towns do," Cap reminded him. "Even Ben Ficklin, sort of."

"But Jake didn't hire them boys from Dodge." I pointed at the shortstop.

Bold black letters spelt LOUISVILLE across his gray shirt.

McKendree come over, so I pulled the scorebook from my war bag and let him pencil in his lineup.

"Got some new boys, I see," Sergeant Searles said.

"Needed a few hands," McKendree lied. Ain't no ranch in West Texas a-hiring no new hands after the gather. Besides, the way the left fielder and pitcher talked, they sure wasn't no Texans.

When McKendree give back the scorebook, soldiers crowded me.

Right fielder Luke Sundee, third baseman June Raines, first baseman Slim Byrne, center fielder Plug Hat Charly, Ray Birmingham on the bench (a limestone shelf), and McKendree a-catching, them we all knowed. Batting second, however, was the second baseman with the C on his shirt, whose name was listed as only Smith. The shortstop, Louisville Louie, batted fourth. The left fielder, Killer Kline, batted seventh, two spots ahead of the pitcher, Ban Higgins. The last two I mention wore them M's on their bibs.

"The New York Mutuals." Cap tapped the crudely written lineup. "The most corrupt team in base ball. Kline and Higgins got kicked off of National Association of Professional Base Ball Players teams the past few years, but the Mutuals signed them anyway. When this National League was finalized in February, however, the chairman wouldn't let those two fiends play for any team."

In pure amazement, we stared at Cap, who, a-seeing our looks, asked: "Doesn't anyone here subscribe to the *New York Clipper?*"

"Tubby O'Halloran oftentimes rings the changes when someone happens to win at his faro layout in Ben Ficklin," Jeremiah Sherman said. "Reckon McKendree wanted to ring some changes, too." Which got nods from other troopers Tubby had paid off in counterfeit script.

"I suppose Louisville Louie and this 'Smith' are of similar stripes." Cap sighed. "But they ride for the Bar J-5 brand now, so they can play."

Ask me, the only thing them professionals ever rid for the Bar J-5 was that buckboard from the bunkhouse to our diamond.

Sergeant Akins give me the names of his starting nine and Trice, which I writ into the book. Cap fished out a gold piece and asked McKendree to make the call whilst the coin was a-flipping. McKendree called heads, which is how it landed, so the 10th batted first.

I didn't even see Higgins's first pitch to Thelonious Friend, who didn't see nothing neither. That crunch, though, must've been heard all the way to Fort Davis. Then come the cussing from the 10th, laughing from the Bar J-5, and Cap's hollers: "Foul balk! Foul balk! Foul balk!"

Friend didn't hear nothing. He lay stretched out across home base, boots in the left-side box and head, already a-swelling up, in the right, the imprint of the ball's laces visible on the trooper's forehead.

Cap pointed a long finger at the hurler. "This is a warning, sir. You cannot deliver a pitch with an overhand throw. Such is not allowed according to . . ." I didn't hear the rule number for Friend groaned, which told me he weren't dead.

"Can he play?" Nodding at Friend, McKendree tossed the ball back to his pitcher.

"Even if he comes to," I said, "he won't be able to see on account of how swole up his head is."

"Then bring in your substitute!" Higgins hollered from the pitcher's box. "And drag the striker into the shade."

Higgins was being funny. Weren't no shade to speak of along the Middle Concho.

Cap explained that rules was rules, so Searles and McTrammick drug Friend to the rock where I sat to do my score-booking, and Trice taken Friend's place.

"High," Trice called out nervously. Which meant, of course, that Higgins had to deliver his pitch across Jimmy Rose's whitewashed haversack that was home base, above Trice's waist but not no higher than his shoulder.

Which Higgins didn't do.

Cussing, I left Friend and my scorebook and knelt beside Trice, who writhed this way and that, a-covering the haversack with dust whilst Cap hollered once more, "Foul balk! Foul balk! This is your last warning!"

Which is when it hit me—not the base ball, I mean, but what McKendree and Higgins was up to.

"Trooper," I whispered to Trice, "you got to finish this game."

Sergeant Akins called me a cruel cuss, pointed out that Trice's left forearm was busted, but I'd learnt enough about base ball back at that Illinois prison camp and in games I had seen played at forts across West Texas. "If he don't get up, you ain't got nine players, so it's you who forfeits—loses—this game."

"If I get up," Trice said, "he'll just hit me again with that ball."

"No," Cap said, loud enough for everybody to hear, "for if any Bar J-5 man throws one more overhand pitch, they forfeit the game in accordance with rule . . ."

Trice managed to stand by hisself, and taken the bat-stick I offered him. Damned if that tough nut didn't step back inside the striker's box whose lines Slim Byrne had to redraw with his running iron after all the writhing done lately.

The smile disappeared from the faces of McKendree, Sundee, even Higgins. With his left arm a-hanging useless but his right a-gripping that heavy bat-stick, Trice told Higgins again, "High pitch."

It got delivered, but underhanded this time.

Trice grounded out, but as he walked back toward the saddle blankets that served as the 10th's bench, Smith called out from second base: "Good at-bat, soldier." Even Killer Kline tipped his cap.

Something else changed in the stump match, too. Mike Searles stood six-foot-two in his stocking feet (and he wore boots)—big for a pony soldier—and his underhanded throws matched the speed of Ban Higgins's illegal pitches. Striking out Luke Sundee wasn't nothing, but Searles got Smith, a real professional, out on four pitches afore June Raines dribbled a ball that didn't roll no further than six inches in front of the haversack, and Corporal McTrammick picked up the ball and walloped it something good into Raines's stomach.

"The striker," Cap announced, "is out." McKendree cursed the gut-clutching Raines for not knowing to run when the ball gets hit. McTrammick helped the poor cowhand up and shoved him toward third base, a-saying, "Take the field, muffin."

If you've read the *New York Clipper* or some other sporting journal, you know that most base-ball games end with scores like forty-seven to twenty-nine, or sixty-eight to fifty-five.

Nobody had scored in the San Angela Stump Match after seven innings. Which ain't that hard to understand 'cause the Bar J-5 was new to the sport and 'cause Searles, after he run away from that Tennessee plantation, learnt to hurl from the Red Stockings' "Count" Asa Brainard in Cincinnati.

Anyhow, the 10th earned the respect of the cheating pro ballists. I mean, in the third inning, when Searles clipped Ban Higgins's mustache with an overhanded throw and taken his warning from Cap, the ex-Mutuals bad man stood up, dusted off his pants, and grinned at the sarge. "I like your style, mister," Higgins told the sarge. Meant it, too.

The Bar J-5 riders learnt that them troopers played sound ball, and the buffalo soldiers begrudgingly allowed that the Bar J-5 nine weren't no muffins, neither.

Because Plug Hat Charly chased down a ball Sergeant Akins whacked so hard everybody figured to be a home run and caught it on the fly. And Raines knocked down a rifle shot from one-armed Trice and recollected enough of the rules to pick the ball up, tag Ray Birmingham's lariat that was third base to force out McTrammick, then throw to Slim Byrne at first for a double play.

Cowhands, soldiers, and professional ballists, you see, respect ornery, tough folks who work, and play, hard.

I'd even allow that nobody would have scored nothing till this very day had Luke Sundee not dropped Wil Bloford's pop fly in the opening of the eighth inning.

Afore that happened, with one out, Cap awarded Akins first base after rightfully a-calling three pitches "balls" as they come nowhere near high nor the haversack. Ask me, Higgins throwed them pitches that way a-purpose 'cause the sergeant had already battered balls this way and that, including one that disappeared, foul, in the river, a-running good after heavy rains, and a-leaving us with only one ball. A-walking Akins appeared to be a savvy move.

And would've been 'cause Bloford popped up. But Sundee dropped the ball. Even that wouldn't have meant nothing much had Luke picked up the ball and throwed it in, but he wouldn't do it on account the ball landed in prickly pear. Which let Akins score the game's first run afore Kline sprinted all the way from left field and throwed the ball, spines and all, to McKendree, who kept Bloford at the third-base lariat. After we plucked the ball clean, Higgins, madder than a nest of rattlers, struck out Diamond Henry and Jeremiah Sherman and would have strangled Luke Sundee had not Killer Kline reminded Higgins of the warning some judge had give Higgins down in Galveston.

But afore Plug Hat Charly got to strike at Sergeant Searles's first pitch in the bottom of the inning, there commenced the most a-yipping and a-shouting you ever heard at a stump match, and all our horses picketed along the river begun a-snorting.

Lucius Redman hollered, "Comanches!" And I yelled, "They're stealing our horses."

Remember, this was 1876, when soldiers and civilians felt a mite wary of Indians after all that happened to Custer's boys, some being right fair ballists, up Montana way back in June.

Through the dust, we seen the last of them raiding devils, and all our horses, on the far side of the river. And we seen our last base ball go a-flying after them and into the Middle Concho, throwed by a cussing Sergeant Searles.

Afore we all walked back to San Angela, Cap pulled out his rule book and quoted: " 'The umpire, in any match game, shall determine when play shall be suspended, and, if the game cannot be fairly concluded'—and this one cannot as we have no more base balls and it's a long walk back to town—'it shall be decided by the score of the last equal innings played . . .' That, gentlemen, means this game is suspended with the score zero to zero. No winners, no losers, but a sound display of base ball played at its finest. You all should be proud."

"It's hard," Ray Birmingham said, "to be proud when you is a cowboy and afoot."

"At least," Jeremiah Sherman said, "y'all ain't gots to report your horses stole by injuns to Lieutenant Bigelow."

Which brung us all back to the War Paint, where I started this narrative, and where I finish it.

Banned professional ballists, ex-Rebel cowhands, and buffalo soldiers sat a-recollecting all the great plays that had happened at the San Angela Stump Match. And when things started to turn a tad touchy oncet folks started a-blaming one another, I asked, "Did anyone else notice that that last Indian looked a lot like Tubby O'Halloran?"

Cap, perplexed, said, "That brave was thinner than a telegraph pole."

Plug Hat Charly barked: "You must be blind, Galloway. That cur was the spittin' image of that sharper. No wonder you called me out at home base in the fifth. I was safe by four rods!"

"And the tracks I found on the riverbank," I allowed, "come from shod horses."

"Wait a minute." Sergeant Akins begun a-thinking, and then a-cussing Tubby O'Halloran for a nefarious scoundrel.

Jake McKendree preached how that nest of horse thieves and pitiful ballists ought to be run out of Ben Ficklin on a rail.

Louisville Louie, Smith, Killer Kline, and Ban Higgins cussed, too, though they'd never heard of Tubby or the county seat.

I ordered another bottle of forty-rod in an Old Overholt bottle, but four ballists expelled from the National League, ten troopers—even banged-up Thelonious Friend and broke-armed Napoleon Trice—of the 10th, and ten riders of the Bar J-5 was already a-taking the ankle express toward Ben Ficklin.

Oncet the beer-jerker brung over the whiskey, Cap said, "I don't recall you scouting for sign after our horses were run off."

I said, "Because I didn't," and filled our glasses.

Like I done mentioned, as a foot soldier, Cap thought pretty good on his feet, even whilst a-sitting down. "Those horses were not stolen," he said, "by Tubby O'Halloran and his b'hoys."

"Nor Comanches," I said. "Lipans be my guess."

Our glasses clinked, and we drained them.

"I guess," Cap said, "the only thing better than a solid game of base ball to bring enemies together is cleaning out Ben Ficklin . . ."

"Together." I grinned.

This time, Cap poured the whiskey.

★ ★ ★ ★ ★

THE SOUTHERN FRONTIER

★ ★ ★ ★ ★

I'm often asked how a kid who grew up in the tobacco fields and swamps of South Carolina came to write Westerns. My answer: Because the West wasn't filled with tobacco fields and swamps. Besides, after having a few autobiographical Southern stories published in literary magazines, I realized that if I wanted to continue receiving invitations home for Thanksgiving and Christmas, I might be better off writing Westerns—even though I've often transported people I knew and events I witnessed in the Pee Dee into Western settings.

Here are a few South-Westerns. The setting might be the South, but they could easily have taken place in the West, too. And sometimes things get real Western in the Deep South.

I AM HUGH GUNTER

"I am Hugh Gunter."

The man doing the hiring pushes back his cocked hat, and stares.

"Your skin be dark, boy," he says.

"I am Black Dutch," I say.

Black Dutch. For two years, I've been saying that. To hide who I really am. Oh, my name's Hugh Gunter. That's what my mother and father wrote in our Bible when I entered this world fourteen and a half years ago in our cabin north of New Echota, Georgia. That's right. I was born in a house. We had a Bible. We raised crops. We read books. We were civilized.

"Make your mark," the man says, and he's surprised when I sign my name.

I can write, too.

But I am not Black Dutch.

We leave Pickensville that brutally hot afternoon, the overseer, four burly white men in buckskins and homespun cotton, and me, all of us wearing moccasins, bound for the farm of a man named Hornsuckle. This rolling country, hundreds of miles from what had been my home, is unfamiliar, but once, belonged to my people. I don't talk much, but I hold nothing against this overseer, or the four white men. They are farmers, trying to make a living in the rough backcountry, and not gold-hungry Georgians who drove me from my home and sent my parents

109

and sisters far to the west.

Two days later, I'm working with the other hands. Sweat stings my eyes. Some men chop down tobacco stalks, splitting them with knives near the base. Others tie seven or eight stalks to a heavy stick, hard as steel after being baked in wretchedly hot barns. These sticks I carry to the barn, handing them to another man, who hangs them in rows to be flue-cured.

Oh, we knew of tobacco in New Echota. Cudweed, we called it, and used it in ceremonies. Here, white men grow it for profit. In New Echota, we raised corn—called selu, the name of our First Woman—beans, squash, pumpkins. My mother and sisters worked the fields. We ate apples and black-eyed peas. We gathered mint, blackberries, ginger, yellow dock, sumac, and hummingbird blossoms. It was a good life.

I work without complaint, or any comment. Hornsuckle is rough as a cob, but pays fair wages, and the food his wife serves us is not hog and hominy. At night, we sleep in a livestock barn, which reminds me of New Echota.

In a barn like this, one night two years ago, my mother and father told brother John and me that we must leave, take to the hills and hide, before the soldiers came to take us away. Before the white men came to steal our home. For years, we knew this day was coming, but never did I think it would truly happen.

"They will send us to Tennessee," our father said, "and from there we will walk to this Indian Territory."

"It will be winter!" I cried.

"We will manage," our father said.

"We will come with you," my brother said.

"No." It was our mother who spoke so sharply. "You and Hugh will stay. This is our country. Your country."

"Maybe," our father said sadly, "one day we will return home." Yet even as he spoke those words, he knew that the white men would never let that happen.

"Hide in the mountains," our mother said. "Others will, too. But if you meet white men, tell them that you are Black Dutch."

"From Long Cane Creek," our father added.

So we ran to the hills to hide. Like animals. The soldiers and white men searched for us, but we knew this land well. After a while, hungry, we ventured back to the settlements, claiming to be Black Dutch, finding odd jobs, doing anything to survive. Yes, soldiers took our family away. Later, we heard that they had gathered maybe 13,000, maybe 15,000 of our people, and in winter, sent them west. Our people called it *Nu na da ul tsun yi*, "The Place Where They Cried." Thousands died on that trail. Our mother? Father? Our sisters? We do not know. We cannot ask.

We are Black Dutch.

At least, I am.

John and I separated eight months ago. A plantation owner offered him a job in Georgetown, so he went toward the coast. "You are fourteen, Hugh," John told me. "You are a man. You must find your own path."

Since then, I have been alone.

Until, that is, this morning.

Hornsuckle and the overseer have caught a boy stealing from the root cellar. They have bound his hands behind his back, and as the farmer's hounds continue to bark and howl, they bring him outside the barn, where, sleepily, we step into the early morning sun to see what has caused such excitement.

The prisoner tries to run, but the overseer, Dunlap, trips him, then lifts him up. The boy, maybe ten, perhaps younger, kicks, twists, but cannot free himself. He says nothing.

He is filthy, but not from the tobacco that coats our hands with black tar. His cheeks are hollow, and he looks as if he has

111

not eaten in days. His long hair is matted from sweat and dirt, his black eyes are wild. He could be Black Dutch, but parts of that stained, ripped wardrobe—the ribbon shirt and calico turban—give him away.

"He's a feisty little Cherokee," the hired man named Mc-Knight says.

"Feisty little thief," Hornsuckle says.

"What you gonna do with him?" the one called Wooten says.

"Kill him," Hornsuckle answers. "Last month, a Cherokee scalp fetched twenty dollars in Pickensville."

The hired men whistle, and Dunlap draws his knife.

"Twenty dollars is not much," I hear myself saying, and feel white eyes boring into me.

"It's a right smart," Wooten argues.

"There is a slave auction in Ninety-Six on Saturday," I lie. I have not been to Ninety-Six in months. "Dirty as he is, young as he is, he still would fetch more than twenty dollars."

The dogs have quit barking. There is no sound. Dunlap stares at Hornsuckle, who lights his pipe.

"How do you know that?" the farmer asks.

Dunlap answers for me: "The kid hails from Long Cane Creek."

Finally, Hornsuckle nods at Dunlap, who sheaths his knife. "You should speak up more, Hugh Gunter," the farmer tells me. "You got a brain in that head of yourn."

It is agreed. Hornsuckle and I will take this Cherokee to Ninety-Six to be sold like a cow or horse. The others will finish with the tobacco crop. McKnight guards our prisoner while we work the fields. After supper, Hornsuckle and I pack food in knapsacks, fill our canteens, sharpen our knives and hatchets. Tomorrow morn, before sunrise, we begin the eighty-mile walk to Ninety-Six. I wonder why I said what I did. I wonder what I plan to do.

The Cherokee prisoner does not talk.

Ninety-Six is the opposite way I must travel.

Awake, I toss off my blanket, and tiptoe across the hay. Wooten is supposed to be guarding the Cherokee, but his snores echo across the barn. The boy is awake, silent, watching me with suspicious eyes. I draw my knife, and slice through the rawhide that binds his wrists.

When I motion for him to rise, he does. Silently, I sign with my hands that he must follow. After grabbing the knapsack, we slip out of the barn, giving the dog pens a wide berth. Then we run.

We do not stop until the sun is high. Reaching into the sack, I pull out cornbread and salt pork. We wolf down the food, washing it down with tepid water.

"I am Hugh Gunter," I tell the boy.

Still, he does not speak.

I am about to say more, when I hear them.

Hornsuckle's hounds.

We run.

The country has become hilly, rugged, murderous. My lungs scream as we reach the top of a ridge. Mosquitoes swarm. Sweat drenches our shirts. The dogs sound closer.

I need water before I can talk, but even then cannot summon the words. With my hands, I motion at the boy's moccasins and pull off my own. From the sack, I withdraw onions. The boy pulls off his moccasins, and watches silently as I furiously rub an onion over the bottoms of my feet. "You, too," I say, handing him an onion.

When we have done this, I ask for the boy's turban. Reluctantly, he removes this from his head. I bundle our moccasins around a heavy stone, and use the filthy calico to wrap it. Finally, I summon all the strength I can find, and send the ball of moccasins, stone, and turban rolling down the steep hill.

With luck, the dogs will follow that, and, with the onions disguising our scent, buy us some time.

We run.

The onions are gone, and our feet are raw from briars, sharp rocks, the bites of bugs. We have traveled thirty miles or more. Our food is gone, but I have found berries, just enough to keep us going. The rolling farmland is an ancient memory. Gone too are the foothills. Now we are high in the mountains, climbing over rocks and boulders, sweating underneath the towering trees. I follow the sound of roaring water. We are lost. Yet we have not heard Hornsuckle's hounds in two days.

Voices reach me, and I freeze. How foolish to think that Hornsuckle has given up. His pride has been hurt, and his pocketbook, and he likely wants me almost as much as he wants this silent Cherokee.

When we reach the river, we step into its swift current. Water reaches my waist, and the boy's chest. The temperature of the forest is bitterly hot, but the water brutally frigid. We move, slipping on the granite, climbing out of the water and over boulders, back into the cold stream, moving down.

Drenched. Shivering. Aching. The last two hundred yards is almost straight down, on slippery granite alongside the river. White water crashes down, drowning out our groans, all noise. At last, we reach the bottom. White water spills overhead, hurting our heads as we slip beneath this towering fall into a small cave. Hidden behind the waterfall, we wait for darkness in these mountains. We freeze. We do not, cannot, sleep.

Morning comes, and there are no voices. Maybe there are,

but we hear nothing but the roaring of the falls. For all I know, those voices were not of Hornsuckle, but some long hunters from one of the frontier settlements. Perhaps I even hid from our own people.

Somewhere they are here, in these mountains. But where?

I point. He stares. We start.

Climbing again, up the mountain, away from the river. Every so often, I look back and down, but do not see Hornsuckle. Do not see any human. The sun breaks through the trees, dries our clothes, or what is left of our clothes. We slip on loose granite. We slide down. Climb back up. Slide down. For every three feet we gain, we lose one, sometimes two.

Now, drenched in sweat, I can see the top of the ridge, two hundred yards ahead. It might as well be 2,000 miles.

We slide again.

My feet are black, swollen, my hands bloody from cuts, my throat parched. I splash a few drops of water into my mouth, then give the canteen to the boy.

"Finish it," I tell him.

He hesitates, but finally slakes his thirst.

"Let's go," I tell him.

"I can't," he says. I stare. These are the first words he has spoken.

"We must," I say.

"I can't," he cries.

My lips tighten. I do not know how I manage this, but I pull the boy to his feet. I grip his wrists, and lift him onto my back. I drag myself, and him, up an inch, six inches, a foot. Carrying him on my knees. Shale slides down the mountain. Overhead, a red-tailed hawk cries out. Or maybe he's laughing at me.

Rocks gouge my knees. My thighs. Once, I slip, and cut a gash across my forehead. Blood mingles with sweat, which blinds me. I hear myself grunting, the rocks tumbling behind me, hear my mother and father telling me . . .

"Just a little further, Hugh."

"You are almost there, son."

I can sense the top. Gripping the boy's left wrist, I let go of his right, and wipe away sweat and blood. I grab a branch, pull. It breaks off, and I fling it away while sliding downhill four feet. Fifteen minutes later, I have regained that lost ground, and grasp a thick vine. Cautiously, I tug. Then harder. And next I am screaming, pulling, my muscles screaming, my heart about to burst, and then I am at the top, and I roll over, lifting the boy up those last few feet.

Breathless, I lie on my back, stare at the trees, the blue skies, and hear my laughter. Because I have climbed to the top of this mountain, and I am still lost, and we have no water, and no food, and we are bloody, and broken, and likely will die soon from starvation or exposure. Beside me, the boy laughs, too. Perhaps our minds are gone.

The boy says, "I am called Martin Sixkiller."

"I am Hugh Gunter," I hear myself say. Then I hear, see, and feel nothing.

Water drips over my cracked, bleeding lips, soothes my tongue, trickles down my throat. A cold hand wipes the dried blood from my forehead. My eyes flutter open.

Hornsuckle. I almost jump, almost scream, but a hand pushes me down softly, and I realize this is not Hornsuckle, not a white man. He wears a turban, too, and his face is as dark as mine, perhaps darker. Other men, and two women, kneel behind him, dressed in buckskins, and other clothing. I even spy a ribbon shirt. Behind me, the boy is talking excitedly to someone, and a silver-haired man with a proud face appears.

"*O-si-yo.*" He greets me in a language I have not heard in ages. Even when Martin Sixkiller spoke to me, he used English, not Cherokee. For years, this tongue I have not dared speak. Gripping my shoulder, the old man smiles. He tells me his name.

I tell him mine. But this time, I speak in the language I first learned, back in New Echota. There is pride in my own voice, and for my own name, and my people.

I am not Black Dutch.

"I am Hugh Gunter," I say, "of the Long Hair Clan."

ELECTRIC FENCES

For years I thought Mr. Rudolph Graham was the brother of Mr. Green Jeans, the good friend of Captain Kangaroo. He looked like Mr. Green Jeans, talked like Mr. Green Jeans, and dressed like Mr. Green Jeans. I once asked him if he had seen Dancing Bear. He laughed, lit his pipe, and said he had and then told me some tale about himself and Dancing Bear.

Rudolph Graham, you see, was probably the biggest liar in the county. He raised pigs and chickens on a 36-acre farm, but Mr. Rudolph had this deep-seated desire to be a practical joker, which he was. Cruel and sadistic. Definitely no friend of Captain Kangaroo, no kin of Mr. Green Jeans.

On Saturdays, Dad and I would haul garbage to Mr. Rudolph's farm, where he had a dump site in the woods, way past the chicken coops. Then we would stop by his house to visit. I always found it fun because it gave me an excuse to get my shoes muddy as Dad and I walked through the slop and hog manure. But I would freeze in my tracks when I came to a small strand of electric wire, and Dad would have to pick me up and set me on the other side. The wire, with a small current that warned the pigs not to go any farther, was no more than a foot off the ground and I could have cleared it easily, but I was sure even the slightest touch would fry me like an egg.

Mr. Rudolph would laugh and tease. "You scared of that fence, boy. Shucks, son, it ain't even on." He would then cluck like one of his hens, whip out his pecker, and urinate on the

118

wire. When he had finished, he would button his fly and say, "Go ahead. It won't hurt." I would turn to Dad for advice, but he too would just smile. So I never pissed on that fence.

Until June 1968.

We stopped one Saturday on our way back from a fishing trip to show Mr. Rudolph our catch. It was late and he was feeding the pigs, so we walked to him. I was determined not to turn yellow this time. I had baited my hook for the first time—one of the first rites to becoming a man among Southerners—and made Dad proud. I wasn't going to be scared of a small wire, fried eggs or not.

Trembling, I stepped over the fence and sighed with relief. Dad grinned and we waded through the muck to Mr. Rudolph. He stood there, dressed in his dirty shirt and smelly overalls, and poured a can of grain into a trough. "Hi there," he greeted. "Been fishin'?"

"Yep," Dad replied. "Sport here caught a nice-sized perch. Didn't you, Sport?"

I nodded. They talked for a bit and then turned to go back to the truck where my perch and Dad's twelve bream awaited Mr. Rudolph's appraisal. We came to the fence and I froze, chewing my lip. Delayed reaction. Once again, I was terrified of being fried. I heard Mr. Rudolph cackle behind me and I took a deep breath and stepped across the fence. I thought I felt one of my pants legs catch the wire and I almost fell into the mud as I hurried my maneuver, but I came across without the slightest shock or burn.

Dad and Mr. Rudolph crossed without incident, and Mr. Rudolph unbuttoned his fly. "See, I told you t'weren't nothin' to it," he said, giving me his Mr. Green Jeans smile. "Now, let's pee on it." He finished unbuttoning, just as he had done some hundred times before.

To my amazement, I found that I had unzipped my pants

and held my own pecker in my hand. I was eager to pass the second rite of becoming a man, but more so to relieve my bladder of the six Pepsi-Colas I drank on the boat. I waited for a moment and it came. Just before I drained my kidneys, I glanced at Mr. Rudolph. He was smiling that down-home-I-won't-hurt-you-Mr.-Green-Jeans look. Trustworthy as a Cub Scout Den Dad.

To this day, I have problems urinating in the presence of others. Oh, I can pee in a crowded bar bathroom after six beers, but, generally, I head for a private stall. I'm sure others have similar problems, but I don't think my reason is shyness. I think it goes back to something that happened in a pigpen when I was six.

You see, I glanced at Mr. Rudolph's face when I should have been looking at his feet.

The son of a bitch was wearing rubber boots.

THE ANTIOCH COUNTY ALL-STAR GAME

First base was the telephone pole this side of the dirt road that connected Route 1 with Route 2. Second base was that well-flattened, dried-up, perhaps petrified, cow patty that had been in that same spot for three years. Third base was sometimes an empty Pepsi-Cola can, but more often Angelina Fulgenzi's book bag, which had not carried a book since third grade.

The ground rules were as follows: Even if the ball landed in the fire-ant mound beyond shortstop, it remained live. The fielder had to get the ball, and if he got stung a zillion times, that was his own fault. He should have caught it to begin with. If the ball cleared Route 1, our left-field fence, in the air, it was a home run. If it bounced over the blacktop, however, you had to fetch it—and pray you weren't struck by a passing car, tractor, or combine—and if it landed in the ditch, you had to get it, too, and hope those water moccasins were sleeping—unless the ball was sucked down into the dark, murky depths. If the ball landed in the blue hydrangeas bush in center field, Judge Henry's front yard, that was a ground-rule double, but you still had to find the ball. Nine times out of ten we only had two, and one would be too waterlogged to play with after landing in the ditch.

And right field? That's where things got dicey, I mean, treacherous. The playing field ended at the woods guarded by one ugly, brutal, impregnable, baseball-eating, man-killing patch of briars that had shredded covers off of baseballs, sheared off

121

fingers, and arms, and unmentionables. We called it "The Green Monster." Once, two summers earlier, a rabbit darted into that thicket, and the terrifying, ghastly screams that followed would remain unmatched until Emi Penny saw *The Beast from 20,000 Fathoms* one Saturday afternoon on Channel 10. It wasn't really a rule, just what we considered reality. If the last ball landed there, the game was over. No one dared try to retrieve anything after it vanished in those lethal, razor-sharp thorns.

Every August, after Little League season ended and right before school started, we, the Center Road Honeysuckles (uh, Mama named us) met the Peniel Brutes in the Antioch County All-Star Game. For as long as I could remember, which went back, oh, five years, the Brutes had murdered us.

Left-handed-hitting Orion Mulholland led the Brutes. That was his gang, I mean team. I hated Orion Mulholland. Oh, hate's a strong word. Let's just say that if Orion's face broke out in spontaneous combustion, I would have put it out with an ax. I played right field, you see, because nobody hit the ball there, except Orion Mulholland. He'd come to bat like Babe Ruth, pointing to me, and rip one that I couldn't catch. He'd killed many balls by sending them into the briars. Others, I had merely misjudged, dropped, flubbed . . . you get the picture.

Orion was bigger than an eight-grader, and meaner than Angie Luttrell's daddy. Orion poured muriatic acid over his Sugar Pops for breakfast. He stole lunch money from *teachers*. He kept a pack of Lucky Strikes rolled up in his T-shirt sleeve (though we'd never seen him fire one up). He rooted for the Clemson Tigers, not the South Carolina Gamecocks. He chewed gum during church. He also had a curveball that could give Billy Williams fits, and a 33-inch Louisville Slugger that packed the power of Daddy's Belgian Browning 12-gauge automatic.

In 1971, Mulholland's Brutes had whipped us, 19-1, before Judge Henry called the game after two innings on the mercy rule, or because he was out of mint juleps.

But 1972, the year I turned 10, was our year. Our Small Fry team had gone 12-0, winning the Lynches River Little League championship, which my .000 batting average (11 walks and one strikeout—bases loaded, dang it) and the error I committed in right field greatly contributed to.

I was the worst baseball player ever born in Antioch County, but baseball remained my true love, and the Center Road Honeysuckles were my team. I was captain. Everybody knew that. They liked me, even if they didn't care much for my athletic incompetence.

1972 was also the year my best bud, Noah Hornig, showed up with his Excalibur, Worth Bat Company's first one-piece, Little League–eligible, aluminum bat. When you hit the ball, it sounded *ping*, not *crack*—which took some getting used to—but it was light as a feather, and balls flew off that bat and sailed a country mile.

So when we met the week before the game at Judge Henry's front yard, to do the old bat-toss routine and determine home team, Orion Mulholland suggested a wager. The winner would get that Worth bat. The loser would announce at Good Sam Elementary School, first thing every morning until Halloween, that the winning Brutes/Honeysuckles were baseball gods and that the losing Honeysuckles/Brutes were lousier than the Antioch County Post 42 American Legion team, winless since 1969.

"You're on!" I shouted.

"Jack!" Noah cried. "No!"

"We can beat them!" I said, and Noah started to argue, but Judge Henry sipped his drink, and said, "Ah, a friendly wager. Very sportin', boys, very sportin'. See y'all here a week from Saturday."

"*Ha!*" Orion Mulholland laughed, and strode off with his second-baseman-henchman Bacilio Tapia, to steal from the church collection plate, or beat up their mothers, or bash mailboxes along Route 2, or whatever thugs of that ilk do on their way home.

Yes, I was confident, dare I say cocky, until we came to practice the Friday before the Antioch County All-Star Game.

"Where's Wesley?" I shouted.

Wesley Richardson was our Hank Aaron, our Stonewall Jackson, Francis Marion, John Wayne, Matt Dillon, and Marcus Welby. He had hit .697 for our Small Fry team, and, as the Honeysuckles' starting pitcher, had been able to hold Orion Mulholland to only three or four home runs each game.

"He went to Florida," said Mallia Lux. What Mallia was doing on Judge Henry's porch on a Friday in August I had no idea.

"What do you mean?" shrieked Jacob Hayes, our catcher.

"I mean Wesley has a cousin who got a summer job at Six Gun Territory near Ocala, and Wesley went there for the week," she said, the Know-It-All.

My heart sagged. Noah's heart broke. He could see his Worth bat being carted off by Orion. Without Wesley, we wouldn't be able to field a full nine players. We'd forfeit, something we hadn't done since 1969 when half of my Honeysuckles, traitors, went to Santee Cooper for a barbecue-swimming party at Mallia's lake house.

"You shouldn't have wagered my bat!" Noah wailed.

Mallia Lux laughed. She always rooted for the Brutes. I still blamed her and her devious ways for that forfeit back in '69.

"Boys." Judge Henry stirred the ice in his tumbler with his pinky finger, "seems to me that y'all need a ringer."

"What's a ringer?" I asked.

The judge sipped his drink. "A ringer is a person who enters a competition under false representations, usually because he is danged skilled at said competition."

"We ain't got no ringer," Noah said.

The judge set his tumbler on the table. "But I have kin visitin' me from out of state. And I can loan my kin to you for Saturday's game, if Ashley's willin'."

"Done!" I said, while Ryan, our shortstop, asked, "But is a ringer legal?"

"It is," Judge Henry said, "on my front lawn." He tilted his jowly face toward the screen door, and shouted, "Ashley!"

Which is when I, too late, remembered that name.

Our jaws dropped dangerously close to the fire-ant mound when Ashley Gillian Holder stepped outside, shoving an orange push-up into her mouth. She wore ponytails, cutoff jeans, and braces.

"She's a girl!" Noah shouted.

I knew that. I knew Ashley Gillian Holder, had just forgotten her name. Four years ago, I had tried to teach her how to play baseball, but when she hit my pitch, and ran to third base, instead of first, I had tagged the telephone pole, called her out, and laughed. She had cracked my tobacco stick—back then, I didn't own a real bat—over my head. Which explains why I wasn't upset when I heard she'd moved to Kentucky.

"Come on!" Mallia called to Ashley. "Let's walk to Miz Roberta's store at the crossroads and get us a snack."

But Ashley Gillian Holder had spotted something that interested her far more than a Grape Nehi and Moon Pie. It wasn't me. She leaped over the wrought-iron railing, cleared the rosebushes, didn't even lose her balance, and raced to Noah.

"Hey," she said, snatching the Worth bat from Noah's hands. "I've heard of these, but never seen one." She dropped into a batter's stance, swung, and would have bashed my brains out if I hadn't ducked.

"Look out!" I yelled, then took my case to court. "Judge, she can't play with us."

125

"You said she could," the judge said.

"But . . ."

"And this is my front yard."

"But she doesn't know how to run the bases."

"I know a lot more than you think, Jack Schelton!" she barked. "I've learned a lot in Kentucky."

"Let her play," Ryan said.

"Or we forfeit," Noah reminded me, "and I lose the bat Daddy got me for my birthday—*thanks to your big mouth!*"

"All right." It would be the Alamo, Little Big Horn, and the 1966 World Series all rolled into one.

The Brutes were home, so we batted first. Orion struck me out. He struck Jacob out. He struck Noah out. He laughed. So did all the Brutes. Of course, most of them were laughing when they saw Ashley Gillian Holder taking practice swings with Noah's bat.

Mallia's brother, Tristan, pitched for us. He got Andrew Hartwell to pop up to Noah. Then Bacilio lined a drive that bounced high off the telephone pole (first base) and dropped, miraculously, into Tristan's glove as Tristan turned around to watch what he thought was going to be a home run. In left field, Ashley Gillian Holder jumped up and down and squealed like a rising fifth-grader girl, "Great catch. That was super. Super-super-super!"

But then Orion Mulholland came to the plate. First, however, he went to our side of the brick steps, and announced, "Hey, Hornig, I'm borrowin' your bat. But just for a while. Because in an hour, it'll be mine."

Noah started to argue, but Judge Henry slurped his mint julep and said, "Sharin' is a nice trait. Very sportsmanlike. Very sportsmanlike. You Honeysuckles are truly Southern gentlemen."

"Strike him out!" shouted Ashley Gillian Holder.

And, to everyone's amazement, especially Orion's, maybe more so Tristan's, Tristan did just that. Probably because that Worth bat was light, twenty-seven tons lighter than that Louisville Slugger Orion had been using since he was paroled out of third grade. His timing was so far off, on the third strike, he spun around home plate (a whitewashed piece of plywood) twice, crashed to his knees, and grunted.

Our next three ballists struck out in the top of the second. But, so did the next three Brutes. Nobody could figure out how to swing that Worth bat. Yet nobody wanted to give up on mastering it and go back to swinging wood.

"This is one excitin' game," Judge Henry said. "A veritable, I say, veritable pitchers' duel."

"What's *veritable* mean, Jack?" Ryan shouted to me.

"Shut up!" I was nervous.

That veritable pitchers' duel continued in the third, when my cousin Vern Carr popped up weakly to Bacilio, and Emi Penny's brother, who couldn't hit worth a nickel, struck out without coming close to the ball. Which brought Ashley Gillian Holder to the plate.

She connected on Orion's first pitch, and drilled that ball, just missing the fire-ant mound, and coming dangerously close to the blue hydrangeas. We cheered like we'd never cheered a girl before. A two-out double. Only . . .

Ashley Gillian Holder never reached second base. She stopped, looking one way, then the other, finally turning toward me and screaming, "Where's second base?"

"It's the cow turd!" I shouted. "Hurry!"

She didn't.

"I'm not stepping on that!" she yelled.

And Andrew tagged her out.

The Brutes laughed at her. So did Mallia, Emi, and Angelina.

Even Jacob. The judge himself chuckled in spite of himself. She fetched her glove off the steps, and instead of going to left field, went right to the mound, which wasn't really a mound, but it wasn't a depression, either, in the judge's front yard.

"Give me the ball," she told Tristan. Her face flamed red. "I'm pitching."

"You are not!" I shouted.

"Am, too," she said.

"I–"

"I'd let her, Jack," the judge told me, and since this was his property, and since he knew what a ringer was, and what *veritable* meant, I told Tristan to run off to left field, and warned him to watch for traffic in case they bounced one over the road.

I'm glad I thought of that. I mean, letting Ashley Gillian Holder pitch. She threw like Steve Carlton.

Down went Brute after Brute after Brute. Unfortunately, with Orion Mulholland pitching, down went Honeysuckle after Honeysuckle after Honeysuckle.

A farmer hauling tobacco had stopped his John Deere on Route 1 to watch. Four Black field hands sat on the trailer and cheered. The Baptist minister pulled over in his Buick, and Judge Henry hollered out if he'd like some sweet tea, which wasn't what the judge was drinking.

"I'm fine, Judge," Preacher Stan said. He stayed until the top of the sixth, but by the time he left, cars and tractors lined that side of Route 1. People sat on their hoods, or in the shade, fanning themselves, watching baseball as they'd never seen it played.

After six and a half innings, Judge Henry asked if we'd like to take a break for lemonade, but we weren't having any of that. This was the greatest All-Star game in Antioch County history. A scoreless tie until the ninth inning when Ashley Gillian Holder sent a fastball from Orion Mulholland completely over Route 1, over the tobacco trailer and the Black workers, in the air, splashing in the ditch next to Mr. Ray Allen's field corn.

"A home run!" Mallia squealed, jumping up on the porch, clapping her hands. "A home run! A home run! A home run! Way to go, Ashley!"

"Shut up!" Orion yelled. "You s'posed to be rootin' for us!"

"It's all right, Orion!" Bacilio yelled. "We'll get that run back in—"

"Shut up!" Orion yelled.

The earth trembled. Ashley Gillian Holder even touched second base.

We waited for some Brute to fetch the ball, but the ditch water had claimed yet another victim.

We had one ball left.

I came up to bat next, and struck out, but not before Orion scared the devil out of me with three balls that came close to knocking my head off.

Now, this is August, mind you, also known as a furnace. A thick, humid, miserable, life-sucking furnace. We were sweating enough to flood the Atlantic Ocean, and after two hours of baseball, felt zapped.

The Brutes came to bat in the bottom of the ninth, trailing 1-0, but they didn't look scared.

Even after Andrew popped up behind the plate. Jacob snagged the ball, didn't drop it even after he crashed into the stack of rusty beer cans that decorated that side of Judge Henry's carport.

"I'm glad the Reverend Stan didn't see that," the judge said, chuckling.

One out.

Bacilio fouled off three consecutive foul balls. Ashley's fastball had lost its zip. Her right arm practically dragged the grass. He fouled off another.

"Wait!" I pleaded with Judge Henry. "Four foul balls and he's out."

"Not accordin' to the rule book, Jack, my boy," said the judge, who went back to sipping his mint julep.

We wouldn't know anything about that. The closest thing we had to a rule book was Noah Hornig's Bobby Richardson rookie baseball card. Bobby Richardson was OK, even if he had played for the New York Yankees.

Bacilio doubled on Ashley's next pitch. The crowd along Route 1 cheered, but only politely. I think they were pulling for us Honeysuckles. Southerners, you see, have this thing for . . . er . . . lost causes.

Orion Mulholland swaggered to the plate, like Mighty Casey, or Mickey Mantle, or Hank Aaron. He held Noah's bat like he owned it. He fouled one off the judge's roof. Didn't swing at Ashley's next pitch, which was wide and low. Her next pitch bounced across the plate. Her fourth, he straightened and almost pulled it fair.

Gulp. Toward me!

Two balls. Two strikes. He fouled another off, closer to being fair, closer to coming to me. Turning, face shining with sweat, Ashley signaled me to come in from my shady spot in right field. I jogged to the mound.

"I'm done," she said, and she looked done, pale—did I mention that she lived way up north in Kentucky, where it never got this hot?—and flummoxed. You could have filled a bucket just wringing sweat out of her ponytails.

"You need to pitch," she says.

"I don't pitch!" I argued. "I play right field. Where they never hit the ball. Unless they're—" Another gulp.

"Pitch," she said. "You can do it, Jack. I know you can. It's just one strike." She didn't wait for me to answer. Just tossed me the ball, and trotted off toward the shade.

"Hey!" I said, but she waved me off. She got into a ready position deep in right, like she was Roberto Clemente.

I looked at Jacob, who signaled me pointer finger–pinky–three fingers twice–thumb. Like I knew what that meant. Like Jacob had a clue. I took a deep breath, came set, let out a breath, and threw the ball that hit the rain gutter over the carport, and bounced off Jacob's head.

"Is that the best you got?" Orion laughed as Bacilio stole third. The tying run at third base. One out. And the greatest sixth-grade slugger in probably the entire South at the plate. Who was due for a hit.

We were doomed. So was Noah's new bat.

I made a perfect pitch. Meaning that it was a strike. And perfect for Orion to smash. Which he did. I turned, nauseous, and watched the ball go sailing far into right field. Well, at least I couldn't drop that one. There it went. Far . . . Far . . .

Then I spotted Ashley Gillian Holder running, making a beeline, jumping, and I heard myself screaming, and heard every Honeysuckles player and four or five Brutes, even Mallia, hollering:

"Not the briar patch!"

Ashley left her feet, and left this world, disappearing in The Green Monster, which had ended many a baseball game, many a life.

Every one of us sprinted to the outfield, sick at what we knew we would find: a puddle of blood, maybe a lock from her ponytail, clothes torn to ribbons, a fingernail, a blue eye, bits and pieces of a grass-stained, bloodstained Spalding baseball without a cover.

At home plate, Bacilio and Orion were dancing, celebrating their walk-off home-run victory.

That wasn't.

Because just like that, Ashley Gillian Holder emerged from

the briars, scratched a bit for sure, her left sleeve ripped, spitting out a green leaf, but holding the ball in her glove, then racing past us, all sliding to a stunned-silence stop. She darted across the slick grass, and stepped on Angelina Fulgenzi's third-base book bag.

"Double play!" she shouted to her great uncle.

Judge Henry did not move. His eyes were closed. His pale right hand gripped the sweaty tumbler. We joined Ashley, and stared at the old man. Cautiously, the Brutes approached us.

"Uncle Henry," Ashley called out, her voice cracking.

Orion spit. "He's dead." And laughed.

"I'm not dead," Judge Henry said. He lifted his glass toward his lips. "Merely restin' my eyes."

"That was a double play," Ashley said.

"Indeed," Judge Henry said. He held up his glass in a toast.

Which brought the Brutes almost up the steps. "What's that, old man?" Orion bellowed.

"Ashley caught the ball for the second out of the innin'," the judge explained. "Bacilio left third without taggin' up. Ashley then touched third base, thus out number three. That's the ball game, boys and girls."

"How would you know, old man?" Orion bellowed. "Your eyes were closed."

"After the play, son," the judge said. "I was merely replayin' the scene again, with my eyes closed, to make sure I saw it right. I did. Honeysuckles win, 1-0."

We cheered. Tractors, Buicks, Methodists, Oldsmobiles, Chevys, Fords, Black men and Baptists pulled back onto Route 1, and drove away. A few honked their horns in salute. They did not get to hear Orion tell the judge just what was on his mind.

"That's my call," Judge Henry said. "As umpire. As judge. And as owner of this here baseball diamond."

Orion spoke some blasphemy.

"Son," the judge said, "you lost fair and square in a game all y'all should be proud of. But the Honeysuckles are the champions of the world . . . for this year."

"Antioch County, not the world," Bacilio said.

Judge Henry sipped his mint julep. "I dare say," he said, "Antioch County is all the world most of y'all will ever know, 'specially if y'all continue to hang out with this reprobate."

"Well, that don't cut it with me," Orion said. "And I'm takin' this bat. It's mine. We won. Fair and square."

That's when Judge Henry pulled a hidden Luger from his waistband, and shot Orion Mulholland dead. Bullet right between his eyes. Then he shot Bacilio. Then he gunned down all of those evil Brutes. He even shot Mallia, just for spite.

Well, not really. He stared. That's all it took. Orion threw the bat to me. Threw it hard. But I caught it. Like I was a major-league player, and on that August day in Antioch County, I sure felt like one.

"Keep your stinkin' bat!" he said, and stormed off.

Bacilio, however, looked kinda sheepishly at me, then Ashley, and said, with a smile, "Good game."

"This'll go down in history," Ryan said.

"They'll be talking about it a hundred years from now," Jacob said.

Noah beamed. "And I get to keep my bat!"

Tristan picked his nose.

"Are you all right, dear?" Judge Henry asked Ashley.

She nodded, and grinned. For a girl, she was all right.

"Golly, that was the greatest catch since Willie Mays's!" Noah said, and we realized it was, though none of us had been born when Willie Mays made his legendary grab back in '54.

We lifted her to our shoulders, and cheered. And the funny thing is, the Brutes cheered with us. Except for Orion Mulholland, who was halfway to Route 2 by then, not to mention juvie in four years.

"Yeah," Andrew said. "That was the most awesome all-star game ever played, even if we did lose."

"No one loses in baseball, son," the judge said. "When he, or she, plays his, or her, best."

He lifted his glass in toast. "You are all all-stars, all champions, each and every one."

MASSACRE AT
CHEST OF DRAWERS MOUNTAIN

Once upon a time in the days before political correctness and cultural awareness, Chief Hornet led his bloodthirsty band of savages against the Shoe-Box Settlement that lay at the base of Chest of Drawers Mountain, slaughtering many brave frontiersmen and abducting a 6-year-old boy before disappearing on the trail that led to the top of the monolithic butte.

Chief Hornet was a Cheyenne, sometimes a Sioux, occasionally a Comanche or Apache, and Chest of Drawers Mountains rose above the plains of Wyoming, or Montana, but usually Texas. Actually, Chief Hornet was one of Mama's hair curlers, his arrows and lances bobby pins, and Chest of Drawers Mountain butted up next to the dresser in the master bedroom of our house.

My parents sat in the living room next door, trying to make out something through the TV static as the wind wailed and rain pelted the house. I was the youngest of four children, but the only kid home that June afternoon. Sisters Ellen and Becky were in North Carolina at church camp, and big brother Graham, Second Lieutenant, U.S. Army, had been in Vietnam almost a year.

After sweeping through central Florida and northern Georgia, former Hurricane Abby, now only a tropical depression, dumped buckets of rain on our farm. I don't remember if my parents fought with the rabbit ears to catch the weather or the latest news on Robert Kennedy's assassination. Whichever, they firmly told me that there would be no TV for me that day—no *Have Gun–Will Travel* reruns, no *Gunsmoke* or *The Virginian* or whatever I was watching in 1968. So I retired to the bedroom and turned my mother's hair items into my own Marx Western playset.

Chief Hornet led his red devils up that treacherous mountain of sheer granite (cherry wood) to the flattop mesa thousands of feet (46 inches) above the Texas plains (hardwood floor). A few of his unfortunate braves, however, slipped on the ledges (brass pulls), screaming as they toppled head over heels to their deaths, bouncing off the floor. Little did the surviving heathens realize they were being pursued by Lieutenant Graham McKey and his company of handpicked soldiers.

Graham McKey was 16 years my senior, a wide gap between brothers, yet somehow despite football, ROTC, cropping tobacco, and cruising for chicks at the Burger Ranch in his Ford Galaxy, he still found time to play with me. He'd be Gil Favor to my Rowdy Yates, Candy to my Little Joe, or Bronco to my Sugarfoot, but usually we made up our own heroes. The last time I saw him, right before he shipped out, he had helped me carve out wagon roads with a hoe on our dirt driveway.

"This is Texas," I told him, and he said, "Of course," and marked the state boundary with a tobacco stick, a wonderful toy that could serve as horse as well as Winchester rifle or saber. We played Cowboys and Indians with plastic figures because Mama would have tanned both of our hides had I taken her curlers outside, until he tousled my hair when we were called inside for supper.

"You'll have to be the man of the house while I'm gone, Sport," he told me.

"Un-uh," I answered. "Daddy's the man of the house."

Graham smiled. "No foolin'." But he really didn't say *foolin'*.

He mailed us one picture of himself from overseas: a 22-year-old in fatigues and beret, holding an M16 at his side and lean-ing against sandbags. At home, Becky watched Walter Cronkite give the casualty reports, Ellen argued with anyone about the injustice of the war, Daddy yelled at her to turn down the stereo, and Mama simply prayed. Of course, while other 6-year-olds fought their pretend battles in make-believe jungles, I stuck to the Wild West.

"Sport," Daddy said, sticking his head in the doorway, "stay away from the window. Wind's pickin' up."

I nodded, irritated at being interrupted just before Lieuten-ant McKey led a surprise attack against the gloating Indians atop Chest of Drawers Mountain. Arrows and lances filled the sky. Cavalry sabers hacked away. Blood spurted to the music of the theme song I hummed. As our house began to moan, Mc-Key grabbed the hostage boy and tossed him to his trusty sergeant just as the fiendish renegade chieftain plunged an Apache-Comanche-Sioux-Cheyenne lance through the hand-some lieutenant's back. The bobby pin skewered the hair curler. I cringed.

Yet somehow, Graham McKey stood. He turned to face a smiling Chief Hornet as the sounds of battle died down. Glanc-ing at the bloody spear point protruding from his chest, the lieutenant half-stumbled, half-walked toward the evil Indian leader. Hornet's grin vanished and he backed away until he stood at the edge of the mesa. He dropped his weapons and pleaded, but on came McKey, who gripped the chief's shoulders and pulled him forward, the lance stabbing Hornet through the heart, pinning both men together.

Then they fell, toppling silently off Chest of Drawers Mountain and landing on Dresser Flats amid the ashtray filled with spare change. Somehow still alive, McKey pulled himself free and looked up.

"We've got the boy, Lieutenant!" the sergeant hollered down.

"And Hornet and his men are wiped out."

Lieutenant McKey smiled, nodded, saluted, and died.

Carnage complete, I immediately walked to the window.

A transformer blew out, the house went dark, and Daddy yelled for me to hurry to the living room.

Abby wasn't much of a hurricane, especially after traveling over land for so long, but the tornado she spawned destroyed our house. I remember the roar, but nothing else until I woke up in the flooded stream behind our house, choked on water, and screamed for help.

"Give me your hand!" Graham shouted. He wore the blue uniform of a cavalry lieutenant, yellow kerchief around his neck, and I reached out for the brother I had just un-Christian-like left dead, albeit a hero. He fought against the current, slipping once, but never let go of me until we reached the bank. Kneeling over me in the rain, Graham smiled, nodded, saluted, and disappeared.

They found me like that, wet and cold with several cuts and a minor concussion, gripping a hair curler in my right hand. Mama bawled, hugging me until she almost choked me, praising God, screaming that it was a miracle. I didn't think anyone could cry that much until two days later when the telegram arrived.

Then, it was me crying. Crying harder than my parents and sisters. Crying that I had killed my brother, at Chest of Drawers Mountain and at a place called Binh Long.

Eventually, the tears ran their course until 25 years later when I stood on the Washington Mall, traced Graham McKey's name with pencil and paper, and left one of Mama's hair curlers at the base of the wall.

Daddy said I must have taken the curler with me right before the tornado sucked me out of the window. But I know I left it on the dresser after the last Massacre at Chest of Drawers Mountain.

★ ★ ★ ★ ★

THE EARLY YEARS

★ ★ ★ ★ ★

Writers have to start somewhere. I started writing short stories for small magazines and literary journals. Short fiction is the best way to experiment.

Here are some early short stories.

Irish Whiskey

We was wintering at old Ben Macrae's way station about a day's ride from Tascosa. Six of us was drinking our way to spring, spending our summer wages. It was the third straight winter I had spent at Macrae's, and it started out about as dull as pulling line riding duty. But the excitement picked up when Sean O'Donnel dropped dead in January.

O'Donnel had ben engaged in some non-Christian act with a lewd woman upstairs when his pump broke, least it was the best Hoyt Brigham and I could figure. We went upstairs after Sarah Mae Mixon come running down hell-bent for leather, screaming like a drunk Kiowa. O'Donnel was on his knees at the foot of the bed, britches around his ankles and trapdoor open on his long johns. His head was on the bed, eyes wide open, lips a deep purple and locked in a weird smile.

We went back downstairs and reported our findings to Macrae, who was busy trying to calm down Sarah Mae. An incident like what happened upstairs could put a damper on business, but then again, it might improve it. After bellying up to the bar, Willie Rogers took over as leader on account that he had the most schooling.

"I reckon the thing to do would be to notify O'Donnel's next of kin," Willie said and poured hisself a shot of bourbon.

We thought it over in silence for a minute. then Red Charlie murmured, "Hell, he ain't got no kin, worthless old reprobate."

After chewing the thought over for a moment, Willie downed

143

the shot and said, "We have to settle his estate."

"Estate?" I said. "That peddler ain't owned no land. He ain't had nuttin cept for that wagon of his."

Willie shook his head. "Estate means all of his belongings, wagon and what's in it—"

"Hell," Lubbock Joe said. "When I was fighting injuns with Genral Miles, we said winner takes all. The spoils of war."

We all nodded.

Then Macrae started screaming in his heavy Scottish accent. Sarah Mae was calmed down now after having six shots of sour mash. "You can divide that bounty all you want. I want no part of that man's business, but I want his body out of here now!" He added a few frails and dressing.

Lubbock Joe and Hoyt walked outside to check the supplies in O'Donnel's wagon, while Red Charlie and I went to haul the dead peddler downstairs. I reckon it was because of the cold, but O'Donnel was perty stiff. I was worried that it would be difficult bringing a corpse down those creaky stairs, but it was just like carrying a piece of driftwood. We took O'Donnel outside and laid him on the seat of his wagon. It was freezing cold and sleeting a little, so we didn't stay to help Hoyt and Lubbock Joe. We was back inside the way station in no time, and a couple of drinks warmed us up again.

Sarah Mae had passed out at the table, so Macrae was tending bar. We was perty anxious to hear Lubbock Joe and Hoyt's report. Most of O'Donnel's merchandise was junk he sold to injuns, but he also had a mighty fine buffalo robe I wouldn't mind having.

Lubbock Joe and Hoyt came flying through the doors like a couple of spooked mares. We poured them some sour mash, and after they downed the stuff, Lubbock Joe stuttered, "Two cases of Irish whiskey. He's got two whole cases of Irish whiskey."

Hoyt nodded in agreement and added, "Most of the other stuff is junk. You know, lard and trinkets and a couple of blankets, some pans and even a petticoat for God's sake. But there's two full cases of genuine Irish whiskey. Damn!" He refilled his glass.

"Don't forget those two mules he got stored in the barn," Willie said.

The news perked us up, but it sure didn't please Macrae. Willie had just suggested for us to go and bring the whiskey inside, when Macrae snapped, "You ain't bringing no Irish whiskey in my establishment. If you wants it, you can have it, but by damn, you'll drink it outside."

"Ben," I pleaded, "it's freezing outside."

"Then take a couple of swigs and you'll warm up. I didn't care for O'Donnel, I hate the Irish, and there will be no Irish whiskey consumed in me establishment. That's me final word on the matter." He slammed the cork into a bottle of sour mash and put it under the bar. "I won't sit back and watch you drink some dead man's whiskey and put me out of business. I put you cowhands up ever winter, don't charge you much for rent or liquor. I serve sour mash, bourbon, and even a little gin, some beer when I can find a keg, but there will never be any Irish whiskey served in Ben Macrae's saloon."

We stared in silence for almost five minutes. Then Willie said, "I reckon we had better bury O'Donnel."

Lubbock Joe, however, shook his head. "That ground is frozen solid. You ain't gonna be able to bury him till spring."

We nodded in agreement. Macrae had cooled off some and was back serving bourbon. We was still thinking to ourselves of a plan to con the old man into letting us drink the whiskey in the warmth of the way station.

Then young Claude Cooper, who hadn't said a word since December, slurred, "O'Donnel was a card-playing pal of the judge's. He might of had wrote a will. Maybe it would be smart to ride to see the judge and have him decide this matter legal wise."

Red Charlie turned and yelled, "Claude Cooper, you're an idiot. There ain't no call—"

But Willie cut him off. "No, Claude is right, much as I hates to admits it. I reckon one of us should ride out and fetch Judge Henry here. He could even help us settle the matter of the whiskey."

I had just pulled a grayback from my hair and ground it into the floor. "Judge Henry's place is an hour's ride from here. It's sleeting. Who is gonna volunteer to ride and fetch him?"

Nobody volunteered so we sent Claude.

We had another shot of bourbon and then Hoyt suggested we ought to go and bring in the two cases of whiskey so it wouldn't freeze. On unison, we looked at Macrae.

Macrae was staring right back at us, holding a bottle of sour mash in his right hand and a bar towel in his left. We could see his knuckles turning white and those cold blue eyes lose their color.

"Bugger off," he said.

By the time Claude got back with Judge Henry, we was all mighty drunk. Hoyt had passed out and Lubbock Joe had gone upstairs with Sarah Mae, who had woke up and forgotten all about O'Donnel. There was two ways to stay warm during the winter and both could be found at the way station. I reckon Lubbock Joe had gotten tired of drinking liquor, and he always was the kind of guy to live dangerously.

Judge Henry walked in and put a pot of coffee on the stove. I could tell he wasn't too pleased at having to ride out in the dead of winter, but he took a shot of sour mash and got right down to business.

"Are you positive the man in question is dead?" he asked.

We looked at each other. "Yeah," Red Charlie said, sort of unsure of hisself. "I mean he looked dead."

"He were stiff as a fence post," I added.

"Where is the body?" Judge Henry asked.

"We put him in the wagon," I said. "Macrae didn't want him in here."

The judge sent me and Willie outside to bring in the body, but we couldn't. He was frozen to the wagon seat. We went back inside, took a shot of bourbon, and told Judge Henry the problem. He immediately came to the conclusion that O'Donnel was stone dead.

"Well," Judge Henry said. "I do have a will of the deceased, but the only requirements he left were to be cremated, and his remains dumped in the Canadian. He was perty drunk when he made out the will, but it's all legal."

"How about the whiskey?" Red Charlie asked. "Macrae ain't gonna let us drink it here."

Judge Henry smiled. "Claude told me O'Donnel had two cases of Irish whiskey." We nodded. "Well, I reckon we can take it to my place. Y'all can ride out there and we'll drink it at my spread."

We smiled, except for Macrae. "I'll take the two mules," he said. That seemed fair so we agreed.

I finally asked, "What do cremation mean?"

"You stupid idiot," Red Charlie snapped. "I thought you had six years of schoolin'."

I didn't say nuttin. I knowed Red Charlie wasn't sure what the word meant neither, just like everbody else there. He was just trying to show off.

Judge Henry smiled. He weren't no real judge, nor a real lawyer. We just called him that because he knowed a lot, and he was the closest thing we had to the law in these parts.

"It means burned," the judge said.

Red Charlie fell to the floor right beside Hoyt, mumbled something, and his eyes rolled back. Claude turned him over on his stomach in case he threw up.

"Reckon we can burn him in his wagon with all that other junk," I said. We agreed.

Macrae's face lit up and he said, "I'll take care of that meself. Always did want to burn that slob." He put on his greatcoat and went outside.

Judge Henry smiled. "Well, now that all that is settled, let's have a drink." He poured us some bourbon and then helped himself to some coffee. He didn't have no need to buy bourbon, I figured. We was gonna have a lot of free Irish whiskey. I thought it was mighty kind of him to buy us a drink, though, and even invite us out to his ranch to share some of the whiskey.

Lubbock Joe walked out of Sarah Mae's room and fell down the stairs. We could hear him breathing, so we didn't bother checking on him.

"Where are those cases of whiskey?" the judge asked.

"Outside," Willie replied.

About that time we smelt smoke, so we staggered outside. Macrae was walking from the wagon, which was burning like hell. He didn't waste no time with that cremation stuff. I leaned against the wall and stared at the blaze.

"Good job, Ben," Willie said, patting Macrae on the back. "How did you get that fire going so fast? What did you use, coal oil?"

Macrae smiled. I was shocked. I hadn't never seen him smile before. "Nope," he said. "Need a drink, you had best come inside."

BLUE NORTHER

Callie Dunlay had little use for Naomi Pierce, especially now that she had lost her mind. But Naomi and her husband, Reginald, were neighbors, and, Callie being a Christian, it was her duty to sit with Naomi for the night. But she didn't have to like it.

"Hell of a time for Reginald to be in La Junta," John Dunlay said as he mounted his horse. "Woman's damned lucky I happened by." Dunlay uttered an oath, swung from his roan, and tightened the saddle cinch some more.

John Dunlay wasn't a Christian, but he was neighborly. It paid to be neighborly along the Canadian River. Knowing Reginald was in Colorado on business, Dunlay and a hired hand had ridden to the Pierces' with a sack of potatoes—an excuse, actually. He was looking in on Naomi because Reginald had asked him to. Naomi wasn't in the house, though; she was in the shed—buck naked and turning purple because it was cold, and would be getting colder once that norther hit—whimpering like a sick puppy. Damned shed was as rawhide a building as he had ever seen. Barely would provide shelter for a jackrabbit. Crazy to be hiding in there.

Crazy.

He had sent the hired man to fetch Callie, then put Naomi in bed and tried to warm her up some. All she did was whimper, though, and now he was going to have to ride to Tascosa and fetch Doc Scarborough, plus send word to Reginald that his

149

wife had—hell, what do you say? Well, maybe Doc Scarborough would know.

"You sure you gonna be all right?" he asked as he remounted.

Callie smiled. "Sure. You just be careful on the trail."

"Hell of a thing."

"This ain't no place for tenderfeets," she said. "I told you they was making a mistake. Told you they wasn't tough enough to last."

"You told me," John said, then spurred his horse into a trot.

Callie poured a cup of coffee and looked at Naomi, pale as a piece of muslin, but no longer whimpering. She was still except for her eyes, which darted every which way, but saw nothing. Callie sat beside the bed and wished she had brought her can of snuff, but the hired man said it was an emergency. Now she was going to have to go through a whole night, maybe two, without enjoying a pinch. She looked at the row of books on the mantel but she couldn't read. Not even the Good Book. Besides, what had Naomi gained from reading? It didn't save her baby girl. It didn't save her mind.

Lord, she wished she had her snuff.

The norther hit at dusk, wailing like a Comanche singing his death chant and causing the house to creak and moan. Callie stood up and walked to the door, opened it a bit. It was going to be a blue norther, she could tell. Rain, sleet, or both would start falling soon. She wondered about John, but didn't worry. He would be all right. He always was.

She turned suddenly, dropping the coffee cup as Naomi ran to the door and quickly bolted it. Ignoring the spilt coffee, Callie walked over to Naomi and forced a smile. "Don't fret none, gal. Ain't nothing to be scared of."

Callie frowned as Naomi began whimpering again, then

slowly eased the young woman back to bed. Earlier in the fall, Naomi had miscarried during a cold front. She hadn't been the same since. Callie had miscarried once herself. A lot of women had. It was hard in Texas, but you went on. Or you left.

Or died.

"Hon," Callie tried, placing her hand on Naomi's cheek, then jerking it off. She was cold as ice. "You gotta be strong, gal. You gotta be strong or you ain't gonna make it. Then, what's Reginald gonna do? I miscarried once. Probably 'cause I fought off a Comanche attack when I was six months along. You get over it. Be strong, gal."

Naomi wasn't listening; she wasn't able to. Callie stood up and went to light a lantern, but the coal oil was low so she decided to wait. The oil was in the shed and Callie wasn't about to go out in the night now. If she waited, maybe the wind would die down.

It saddened her she couldn't talk to Naomi about the Comanche attack. She loved telling how she, alone, had fought off a horse-stealing party—and her six months pregnant. Course, she had lost the baby, but that was all right. She figured there would be other chances—it bothered John more—but there weren't. Doc Scarborough had said she messed up her insides and wouldn't be having any children. But that was all right, too, though she never would tell John.

She cleaned up the coffee and put another log on the fire, hating having to be here, alone, with a woman who never should have left St. Louis.

Naomi woke up screaming the moment the sleet pelted the roof. Callie ran to her, tried to soothe her, but those eyes were wild with fright, darting left and right. Reginald would have to send her away, and then he wouldn't want to stay. He didn't have it in him.

Callie caught herself. She was happy.

Naomi was silent now, and the cabin was quiet except for the crackling of wood in the fireplace and the pounding of sleet outside. The quietness, however, made Callie uneasy. The fire didn't provide enough light, and Callie didn't like staying in a dark house with a crazy woman. A woman whose eyes just moved rapidly. At least she wasn't screaming, Callie thought, as she put on one of Reginald's greatcoats. "Naomi," she said, "I'm gonna run to the shed to fill up a couple of lanterns. I'll be back in a jiffy."

Naomi's eyes only darted.

Callie shook with cold as she poured the coal oil into the lanterns, then lit one. Reginald's greatcoat provided little warmth from the wind and sleet, even in the shed. She finished her chore, then ran to the house, setting the lanterns on the porch as she tried the door.

It was bolted.

Fear shook her worse than the cold. Naomi must have bolted it after she left. The crazy girl! Callie thought, then screamed, "Naomi! For God's sake let me in! I'll die out here, gal! Open the door!" She banged on the door viciously, screaming above the wind, then tried the windows, but the shutters had been bolted since she arrived. She stood at the corner of the house, looking around, trying to think. The shed? No good. Not enough shelter. Her horse in the corral? She never would make it to her ranch. She needed to stand over a fire. Now.

"Naomi!"

John Dunlay rode beside Doc Scarborough's buggy, the horses' hooves crunching the icy ground. It was mighty cold, but at least the wind had died down and the sleet had quit. They topped the ridge overlooking the Pierce spread and stopped, unprepared for the sight below. Dunlay recovered first and spurred his horse into a gallop.

He swung off his mount and ran to his wife, shivering over an empty can of coal oil. "Callie? What happened?" he said, then looked at the charred ruins of the Pierce cabin, barely smoking. Doc Scarborough pulled up, looked at Callie, then stumbled through the burned cabin and gagged at the sight in the bed.

"Got to stay warm," Callie mumbled through chattering teeth. "Got to stay warm." John knelt beside her, put his right hand under her chin, and lifted Callie's head to look into her eyes. Her eyes only darted.

Gun on the Wall

The marshal? No, he ain't here. Went to Blue Ridge. Can I help you? I ain't no real deputy—used to be, but that was ages ago, long 'fore you was born—but I watch over the place when Marshal Statler leaves town. McGant's the name. John Mc-Gant. Glad to meet you. Well, Marshal Statler should be back in an hour or so, if you'd care to wait. There's coffee on the stove and beer in the icebox. Help yourself. No, no beer for me. You might could say I'm on duty.

Where you from? St. Louis, boyhowdy. Me, I ain't been no-wheres much 'cept Oklahoma—and that was when it was the Indian Nations. Now, that's aging me some, ain't it. Huh? Oh, all my life. Was born on a ranch outside Tascosa, and you prob-ably ain't ever heard of that town, but it was a wild place when I was a colt. Ain't nothing left of it but cactus and rattlers. 'Bout all that's left of this town.

Huh? Gun? Oh that gun. No, Marshal Statler ain't worn a gun—that same gun—in 30 years. You ever seen one of those before? Here, let me show you. It ain't loaded. Doubt if it would fire anyways. I used to take it down and oil it and clean it when the marshal was out of town, but I ain't done that in years. Gun belt's kinda stiff now. He got it special order all the way from Kansas City when he was first elected. Black leather, tie-down holster. Ha, you should've seen him when he first put it on. I joked that he was advertising a leather shop. Gun's a Frontier Model single-action Colt .45. Wood handle, blued. The whole rig costs him a month's wages when he bought it. Only fired it once.

Why does he keep it on the wall? As a reminder, I guess. On second thought, I think I'll have me a beer if you want to know why Marshal Statler keeps that gun belt and Colt on that nail.

Frank Statler was just a button when he was elected, but he was kinda like a local hero, him having fought in the war with Teddy Roosevelt. I think he stayed on the beach the whole campaign, but this town was booming and wanted a hero for a marshal. Frank filled the bill. Me, I was a few years older, and we had worked on this cattle outfit along the Canadian for a while and got to be good friends, so he made me his deputy. He got paid $3 a day, and me $1.75, plus fines and expenses, and that was pretty good wages for a couple of former cowhands. Well, I'm kinda rambling on, ain't I? Used to never talk hardly; now it seems folks can't get me to shut up. Part of getting old, I reckon.

Anyways, it all started when Frank got that gun. He had this old Smith & Wesson .44, but when he saw the gun belt and rig in this mail-order catalog, he just had to have it. Kinda like a kid seeing candy in a jar. So he saved his wages and bought it, buckled it on, and was dressed for Easter. Yessir, he was something proud of that gun. He went to the Canadian Saloon to show it off. His brother, Jed, teased him, pretending to quick-draw him, all that dime-novel stuff. It was a lot of fun, but that was all the celebrating.

That night, you see, somebody broke into Dottie Clarke's mercantile and robbed the place and murdered her—butchered her is more like it. Doc Ziegler said she had been stabbed more than fifty times with a garden spade. I never been so sick in my life when I saw her. The work of a madman. Only a crazy man would do that to a 60-year-old woman. But the killer left that spade sticking in her, so there weren't much doubt as to who done it. Everybody in town knowed whose spade that was. So, Frank and me rode to Aaron Walker's farm. Aaron was an old colored boy, real quiet and kinda friendly, who had a gift with gardening. You ain't from around here, but let me tell you growing flowers in the Panhandle ain't no simple chore, what with the wind and heat and little rain. But Aaron had the prettiest roses I ever did see. In fact, he was working in his flower bed when we rode up, digging with his hands.

"Morning, Marshal Statler, Deputy," he greeted, brushing off his hands on his jeans.

"Aaron," Frank said right back, kinda cheerful, too. "You need a hoe or something for the work you're doing, don't you?"

"I declare, Marshal Statler, if you ain't telling the truth, but I up and lost my garden spade. What brings you out this way?"

Frank cleared his throat and dismounted, and I could see the frightened look come into Aaron's eyes when Frank told him everything.

Aaron was scared to death. He had seen his daddy lynched when he was a baby, and I reckon he thought we was gonna string him up even though there weren't no trees around. "Marshal Statler, I swear to the Lord I ain't done that. I been right here all night and day working in the fields."

"Anybody see you?"

"No, sir, Marshal Statler. I ain't seen nobody in a week 'fore you come."

"Aaron," Frank said, kinda awkward. "I'm gonna have to ask you to come back to town with John and me. Likely, we'll clear this up, but I think it'd be best."

"Yessir, but, well, who's gonna look after my roses? My crops?"

"Oh, I'm sure they'll be all right, Aaron. We should be able to straighten this whole thing out in a day or so." I ain't sure if Frank believed Aaron or not, but I knowed why he wanted to bring him back to town. Both of us had been with old man Potter when he strung up Luke Martin in '96. A lot of folks still believed the best justice was with a quick rope.

It was around noon when we got back, and already a crowd was gathering at the Canadian. Old man Potter's horse was there, and that kinda scared me, Frank, too, probably. I think everybody was scared of Potter. We were almost to the jail when Jed Statler stepped out of the saloon and seen us. "They're bringing him in!" he yelled, and Frank swore underneath his breath. About a dozen men, including Potter, was heading our way. Whiskey and anger ain't a good combination.

Frank told me to lock Aaron up, give him some coffee and a little to eat. Then he added softly, so Aaron couldn't hear, "And bolt the door and don't let anyone in until I say so."

"Yessir," I said, and those were the first words I'd spoken all day.

Frank was standing on the boardwalk, thumbs hooked in his gun belt when I closed the door. I bolted the door, locked Aaron in the cell, and gave him some coffee, then hurried to the door to listen. I was so scared I forgot to fix something to eat, but I doubt if Aaron was all that hungry. Potter was talking when I got to the door.

"What did he say?"

"Said he lost his spade, said he didn't kill her."

"That lying darky!" someone yelled.

"What do you intend on doing about it?" Potter asked.

"My job. This man is going to get a fair trial," he said, raising his voice so all could hear. "Now, why don't all of you go home. There's been enough trouble for one day."

"You leave him to those Yankee lawyers, and you know what'll happen. It'll be just like Luke Martin. They let him go, and he kept on rustling. Till I stopped him." Potter's next words were harsh. "You remember that, don't you, Statler?"

"I remember," Frank said, barely loud enough for me to hear.

"We ought to hang that sumbitch," somebody else shouted.

"A rope ain't good enough for the likes of him. We ought to give him the same he gave Miss Dottie!"

"Anybody mentions killing him again is gonna have to deal with me. Now, I'll say it just once more: Go home!"

Potter spoke again. "You didn't say that four years ago."

"No, I didn't, Mr. Potter," Frank said bitterly. "But I should have."

"What do you mean?"

"I mean I don't intend on making the same mistake again." His voice was raised again. "Now, go home! It's spring. You got cattle to brand and crops to tend to. Leave the law to me. If Aaron Walker is guilty, he'll be sentenced accordingly. If he's not, then I'll find the man who did it. And God help him when I do."

Slowly, they walked away, and Frank told me to open the door. Frank never was much of a cusser, but he swore a little when Potter, Jed, and a few others went back into the saloon.

Frank unbuckled his gun belt and hung it on that nail. Neither of us felt much like eating, so we drank some coffee, then questioned Aaron some more. Like I said, we were both kinda young and scared, but when a person is killed, you can't hides in the office all day. Frank told me to keep the door bolted and not to let anyone in—not Jed, not Doc Ziegler—until he came back. That afternoon was the longest I'd spent, but I knowed the night would be longer. I kept peering out the window, and more and more folks was coming to the Canadian. I could hear Potter shouting, sometimes Jed, and I was getting mighty worried about Frank when he finally came back around dusk.

"Norther's blowing in," he said. "Getting cold."

"Find anything?" I asked.

"Nothing," he said. "Talked to Doc Ziegler, went over to the mercantile, checked the roads leading out of town for sign. Nothing. This norther is gonna wipe out any tracks we might could have found." He glanced out the window. "Gonna be a long night," he said.

All through the night, we made regular trips to the window, looking at the saloon, listening. The more whiskey they drank, the louder they got. Frank said if we got through the night, we'd be all right. But it was a long way to dawn. And by eleven o'clock, I was thinking I wouldn't live to see sunrise.

They were coming, Potter, Jed, maybe fifteen–twenty others, carrying lanterns, whiskey bottles, guns—and a rope.

This time, we both swore. Frank buckled on his gun belt and chambered a sixth round. You see, you kept the cylinder under the hammer empty 'cause it might go off accidentally. I remember when Cherokee Joe first got his Colt and put in six shells. He was riding along, and his cow pony stepped wrong, jarring Joe, and his gun went off and shot off his big toe. There I am wandering again. Anyway, when you put in a sixth shell, you was either loco or meant business.

I grabbed a scattergun, and Frank and me stepped outside.

Jed, Potter, and Eli Carter, who had worked in the mercantile, stepped forward. The rest kinda held back, holding lanterns, guns. The temperature had dropped maybe twenty-five degrees and the wind was howling like the devil. Potter had to shout just so he could be heard.

"We've come to take that murdering dog, Statler," he said. "Get out of the way!"

"All of you, go home!" Frank ordered.

"Not till we get what we come for," Carter said. "This town is growing, but folks—and especially businesses—ain't gonna come to a place where an old white woman can be butchered by a jim crow!"

159

"And they won't come to a place where people take the law into their own hands! Go home! I don't want to use this gun."

Potter laughed. "You gonna shoot your own brother, Statler?"

Jed stepped forward, his arm hanging by his old Army .45. For a minute, you couldn't hear nothing except for the wind howling, jackets flapping in the night.

You have to understand, Jed and Frank loved each other as any two brothers would. And here they was, arms hanging loosely by their pistols, eyes hard and narrow. I tried to swallow, but couldn't.

"You plan on using that gun, Jed?" Frank asked.

"I'd rather kill my own brother than have him called a lover of nig—"

And they drew. It was almost as if the wind stopped for a second, like God was waiting to see what happened. Jed didn't have a chance; he hadn't cleared leather by the time Frank had his gun cocked.

Whoa! There's the phone. Excuse me. . . . Now, where was I? Huh? No, that ain't the end. I kinda wish it was. Truth is, that's only the beginning. You see, I couldn't let Frank kill his own brother, couldn't stand to see what that would've done to him. I coldcocked Frank with the butt of my shotgun. See where the sight is rough? That's where he dropped the gun.

Yeah, I let them have old Aaron, him howling like a coyote, screaming, begging for mercy. They—no, I was there, too—we took him to that big tree at the edge of town. Huh? Yeah, that's the tree. Tornadoes have been through here, ripped up trees, houses, barns, silos, but that tree is still there. Like Aaron's roses. Growing stronger, bigger, kinda haunting us—or maybe it's God punishing us for what we done. We strung Aaron up that night. Only problem was, Eli didn't let the horse out quick enough. The fall didn't break Aaron's neck. He was kicking like a crazy man when Frank got there, the rest of us too sick to do nothing. Frank was dazed, bleeding a little. He didn't say a word. He just cocked his gun and put old Aaron out of his mis'ry. Then he went back to the office and hung up the gun.

Been there ever since, 'cept for the times I'd clean it. Finally, I quit doing that. Well, I'd better put it up. He'll be back anytime soon.

You know, we really thought this town was going to be something. Look at it now. In twenty-five years, there won't be nothing left 'cept for that tree and Aaron's roses. Marshal Statler could've arrested us, but he didn't. Never said a word about it. 'Cept once a year, he drives to the Blue Ridge Cemetery to put roses on Aaron's grave.

Yeah, we hung poor Aaron. I don't know if he done it or not. It don't really matter. 'Cause Jed, Frank, me, this whole town really, died that night.

I guess that's why we keep this gun on the wall.

CRAWFORD MCGEE

What follows is a tale of murder. Whether the act was justifiable remains to be seen, and judgment should be left to God, not the law. I have no respect for the law of Arizona Territory.

Crawford McGee is the reason I shun the law. He was a killer, worse than a two-bit squat assassin, whose guns had claimed the lives of eleven men. Maybe more, because McGee didn't count, in his own words, "greasers and Apaches." Crawford McGee also was a deputy U.S. marshal.

But nothing was righteous about his well-planned executions. He would berate and threaten his target until the latter made an ominous move for a weapon, and McGee, with his badge shielding him, would methodically kill him. With one exception, I am not concerned with the men McGee gunned down. Most of them probably deserved to die. The one I care about is a half-breed Navajo named Charley Quo, a hardworking former scout McGee murdered.

Charley Quo was my father.

I was barely eleven when my father got into a fracas in Sweetwater, knifing a cardsharp from Texas and breaking a bartender's jaw. That was typical of Dad. Even when he was scouting for the Army, he was getting in trouble. After he married Mother, he settled down some, but once in a while, when he would go to town for supplies, he would drop in Harry Chelsea's place for a few drinks and wind up in jail or trouble. Mother would shake her head, pay the fine, and scold Dad in a sharp Scottish dialect. Being a schoolteacher, she could throw out some big words that Dad didn't understand, but they made an impression—at least until the next time he went to Sweetwater.

It was late July when Crawford McGee and another deputy rode to our place along the Gila River. Eyeing them briefly, I returned to playing while they dismounted. Lawmen, soldiers, and ranchers often called on my father, wanting him to scout, guide, or pay a fine. McGee called for my father, and the younger deputy brought the horses to the watering trough near me. I never saw what happened, and Mother refused to tell me, but I can guess. Hearing a bloodcurdling scream, I closed my eyes, knowing what would happen and not wanting to see. I heard three shots and looked to see my father, bleeding profusely from his abdomen, drop an ax. It was three hours before he died, and it wasn't in peace.

Mother died four years later, and, taking her maiden name, I began scouting, usually for the Army, sometimes for the law. In a few years, I had a reputation as one of the best trackers in the territory. Often, deputies and soldiers would ride to my place near Tucson to request my services.

It was a few days ago that Crawford McGee came looking for me. I stepped from my adobe *jacal* to face him, six-foot-four and 220 pounds of hate sitting on a big gray dun. Temples pulsating, I clenched my fist and felt my face flush, then took a couple of deep breaths to regain my composure.

"You Johnny Chisholm?"

Eyes fixed on the six-point star on his dirty cowhide vest, I replied, "Yeah."

"They told me you were part Apache. Don't look it much." I had my father's hair and eyes, but my mother's complexion, tanned from the desert sun but not as dark as most Indians, even those with just a little Indian blood.

"My father was part Navajo," I said, "not Apache."

McGee spit out his cigar, withdrew a warrant from his vest pocket with his left hand, and continued. "I'm Crawford Mc-Gee, deputy marshal, and I got a warrant for Benito Callado. Need a tracker. Pay's two dollars a day."

"What did Callado do?"

"Don't see how that concerns you, but he cracked an ax handle over a whiskey drummer's head, then stole a horse last night in Rillito. Mount your horse, boy, I don't plan on spending all summer with the likes of you."

There was no anger in me. It was early July, one of the hottest years I could remember, thirteen summers after my father's murder and a matter of days before I avenged him.

We picked up Callado's trail around the Sierra Tucsons. I figured Callado would consort with a strumpet he knew around the Maricopa Divide, then light a shuck for Mexico.

It was hot, the wind turning the desert into a blast furnace, but we kept moving on, gradually, not pushing our horses, speaking little to conserve our energy. We had nothing to say to each other. After resting our horses for a couple of hours that night, we moved on.

McGee had a few extra pounds around his middle and some more gray in his hair, but he had changed little since the time he killed my father. He was as hard as the Winchester rifle he carried. His skin, tanned and dried by the sun, was almost as dark as an Apache's, somewhat ironic that he could have been mistaken for one of the Indians he hated. His eyes, however, were pale, a colorless blue that matched his faded jeans. He sat tall in the saddle, a mounted rock, ignoring me. He was a man, I thought, whose only emotion was hate.

We arrived at Carmen Manuel's shack a little before dawn,

smelling the wood burning in her stove long before we reached her one-woman brothel. I waited on the ridge with the horses as McGee went ahead on foot with his Winchester. The sun was slowly climbing over the mesa when my horse whinnied—and was answered by a stallion in Manuel's corral. McGee took cover behind the well; he had heard the horses and was waiting to see if anyone in the adobe shack had. His wait wasn't long.

Benito Callado, wearing only his long johns and a holster, kicked open the door and fired a couple of shots at nothing, then ran for the corral. McGee fired, the bullet splintering a fence post as Callado hurdled the top rail. The second shot killed Carmen's mule as Callado leaped on his bareback stallion, kicked him into a gallop, and hurdled the fence. McGee slowly raised his rifle, and I'm confident his shot would have been true had not Carmen slapped his arm with a frying pan. The slug dug into the Arizona sand, and McGee turned savagely as Carmen screamed in rapid Spanish and silenced her with the rifle barrel.

I brought the horses to the well and let them drink, helped Carmen to the shack, gave her a shot of tequila, and put her to bed. Her left eye was already swollen, and I think her nose was broken. I was going to the lean-to to get some oats for our horses, but McGee was mounted when I came out.

"Leave that whore alone and come on," he ordered.

I thought about arguing, but knew it would be useless. So I tightened the cinch and mounted my pinto. The desert would be the perfect place to commit murder.

We had water; Callado didn't. And in the summer heat, with Callado running scared, it wasn't a long trail. We found his horse three days later, Callado on the fifth afternoon.

Struggling to climb a ridge, Callado turned and panicked when he saw us. McGee, teeth clamped on a cigar, Winchester cradled in his arms, waited. Insulting the hysterical, dehydrated fugitive in Spanish and Apache, McGee seemed to enjoy his work. I saw Callado raise his gun, although we were out of pistol range, and heard the hammer click on McGee's rifle. I don't know what came over me, but that wasn't Benito Callado I saw raising his gun, but my father. Without realizing what I was doing, I found my pistol in my hand and was turning to do what I couldn't do when I was eleven.

"No!" I shouted.

The rest is somewhat vague. I saw McGee reverse-grip on his Winchester and swing the barrel, then felt a crushing blow across my temple as my own gun fired. There was blackness, a blazing pain in my head as I fell. I heard hoofbeats, a horse groan, a pistol shot, a rifle's retort. Three shots, and I saw my father again, screaming and coughing up blood as Mother held his hand, Crawford McGee and a young deputy in our kitchen, drinking our coffee, waiting on Charley Quo, an honored Army scout, to die.

When I came to, I felt as if someone had buried a war ax in my head. I reached to test the knot on my temple and noticed the handcuffs, almost biting into my wrists. Slowly, awkwardly, I sat up and saw Benito Callado, a bloody hole where his nose had been, eyes open. His ears had been sawed off.

"I ought to kill you," McGee said.

I was surprised to be alive, but I spotted McGee's dead horse, his canteen crushed by the saddle horn, and realized where my bullet had struck, what had happened. My horse had run off, probably back to Carmen Manuel's place, taking our water.

"We need water," McGee said. "Get me to a water hole, and I'll let you live. If you don't, we both die, and if I think I'm gonna drop, I'll kill you myself. You better hope I live to see water."

My head, still splitting, was somewhat clear. I was being

forced to save the life of the man I had sworn to kill, but I, too, was thirsty. I knew McGee would kill me soon after we reached the water hole. There were two water holes, Tonto and Culebra, only a mile or two from each other, both closer than Carmen's shack. But a long, hot walk from where we were.

"Gets up," he told me.

"It's crazy to walk through the desert in the day," I said. "Wait until it gets dark."

"Gets up," he said, drawing his pistol.

We walked until I dropped from exhaustion that night, then got an early start the next morning. My tongue was swollen, lips parched, and I kept thinking of the tales of men drinking their own blood, sweat, and urine, eventually dying anyway. I was certain I would die, but I had to outlast McGee. We sat down to rest and he started talking, eyes wild, hands clasped on his gun.

"We were crossing the desert, Ma, Pa, me, and Willie, who had been Pa's slave. Pa freed him after the War, but Willie stayed with us as we headed for California." He laughed. "Mescaleros jumped us, had us pinned down, and that night Pa sent Willie to Fort Bascom to get help. That lousy crow never came back. They hid me in a barrel, and I remember hearing the screams, praying those red devils wouldn't look in the barrel, wouldn't burn it. They didn't, and the next day a couple of hunters found me. I saw Ma, what them savages done to her. And Pa." He laughed again, and I started to get up, but he aimed his pistol at me and cocked it. "Sit down, you lousy injun or I'll kill you just like I did old Willie." Another laugh. "Yeah, I found him a few years later, working for the Southern Pacific, laying track. I gave him the same thing them savages gave Pa."

Pushing on, we stumbled and staggered until we dropped at sunset. I was asleep within minutes, and the next thing I knew McGee was kicking me in the side, the sun burning my neck. I struggled to my feet and we continued, not talking for by then our tongues were too swollen. I have no idea when we reached Tonto Well, or how I found it. It was a fairly large hole, but with no plant life, no animal trails, it was easy to miss. I was lucky. McGee pushed me down, dropped his gun, and ran for the hole. I rolled over and was still, smelling the water, hearing Mc-Gee moaning with pleasure, as I slipped into unconsciousness.

It must have been pushing dusk when I woke. I stuck Mc-Gee's Colt in my pants, removed my bandanna, and stumbled to the water hole. I placed the bandanna in the water, then wiped my face, the water burning my cracked, bleeding lips. I made a cup with my hands, filled it with water, and washed the back of my neck. Then, carefully, I put water in my mouth, swished the bitter liquid around some, and spit it out. I splashed some more on my face and went to find Crawford McGee.

He was some hundred yards from the well, writhing on the ground like a rattler. I reached into his vest pocket, found the keys, and freed myself from the handcuffs. He looked at me, tried to speak but couldn't, then his eyes cleared, understanding. His lips mouthed, "You knew."

Smiling, I nodded. Crawford McGee was dying.

"Mercy," his lips moved. "Kill me."

"No," I said. My voice, dry and cracking like an old man on his deathbed, shocked me, and a minute passed before I could speak again. "Culebra Springs is just a mile from here. Its water is cold, sweet. You'll be dead by the time I get there."

He looked at me, his eyes pleading, but I had no pity. My smile vanished.

"Charley Quo," I said. "Charley Quo was my father." His eyes were uncomprehending when I turned to leave. He couldn't remember Charley Quo, but I knew the name would be on his lips when he died.

★ ★ ★ ★ ★

As I said at the beginning, whether the death of Crawford Mc-Gee was justifiable is in God's hands. Whoever finds this can know I have no remorse. My Indian stamina helped me reach Culebra Springs early that night, and finding this paper and pencil in an old carpetbag, I decided to record my tale. Crawford McGee is dead now, but I'm sure soon we'll both be shouting at the devil.

Tonto Well was poison.

Culebra Springs was dry.

★ ★ ★ ★ ★

CIVIL WAR TALES

★ ★ ★ ★ ★

Dee Brown's Bury My Heart at Wounded Knee *was probably the nonfiction book that truly showed me the power of nonfiction. Of course, Brown's book changed the face of Western literature and much of this country's attitude toward the plight of American Indians. Bruce Catton's* A Stillness at Appomattox, *one of the landmark books about the American Civil War, was another nonfiction book I cherished. I've written a number of Civil War–set novels and short stories, but before you blame this on my Southern heritage, let me point out that Great-Grandpa Daniel Boggs hailed from Illinois, served under General Grant, fought at Shiloh, and named his son Orris Ulysses. Considering Granddaddy's name, I'm thankful that Great-Grandpa Daniel wasn't my daddy.*

THE WATER BEARER

The bullet buzzed past his ear, whining off a rock behind him, and Richard heard his best friend screaming, "Come back!"

Another rifle roared, and this shot came closer to his head. Sure, he wanted to turn and run. No one would blame him, either, standing on open ground, with thousands of enemy soldiers waiting at the foot of the hill. Richard carried no weapon, just several canteens.

"Come back," Denny McBride hollered, "before they kill you!"

Shaking from the bitter cold, Richard could see the rifles aimed at him. He told himself he had a job to do, and uncorked a canteen.

For Richard, the battle had begun after the last shots had been fired the previous day. His stomach seesawed, and he shivered as December's bitter cold engulfed him. The temperature would only plummet now that the sun had begun to sink.

"Battle's over," Denny told him. "Reckon we whupped 'em good!"

His mouth tasted like gunpowder, he longed for water, and Richard could only nod in reply as he rammed another charge down the hot barrel of his rifle.

Battle? It had been *slaughter.* Time and time again Union soldiers had charged the Confederate Army's strong position, only to be driven back until thousands of blue-coated bodies covered the frozen Virginia ground.

"Water . . ." came a haunting plea from beyond the wall. "Mercy . . ." Another beg echoed, then another, and another, the cries pricking at Richard's body like the unforgiving wind. He pulled his rifle closer, trying to block out the sounds.

He hadn't joined Kershaw's Brigade for this. When he had left his farm in Flat Rock, he thought war would be glorious, an adventure any teenager would cherish. Now, he felt as if he were living a nightmare.

"Water . . . please . . . just one sip of water . . ."

He couldn't sleep, not with those wails piercing the darkness, stabbing at him. Never had he heard anything so piteous. Never had he felt so helpless.

When the sky began turning gray, he made up his mind to see the captain, to ask permission to bring water to the wounded men on the other side of that stone wall. Denny told him he was plumb crazy, and the captain agreed, refusing Richard's request, saying he wouldn't risk being court-martialed "for getting one of my boys killed on a fool's errand!"

Head bowed, Richard tried to think of another argument, but Denny tugged his coat, and, silently, led him back to the wall and the tormenting cries.

"You tried, Richard," Denny told him. "Did your best."

No, I haven't done anything. Carefully, he peered over the wall, but saw only a heavy fog. Another voice begged, and Richard knew who might grant his request. He quickly sought Colonel Kennedy, a friend of his father's. So certain he felt that the colonel would say yes that his heart sank when Kennedy gripped Richard's weary shoulder.

"It is a brave thing you ask, son. Alas, I cannot take responsibility. I would loathe writing your father of your senseless death."

Richard bit his lip. Still, he couldn't give up. "Would you

grant me permission to ask the general?"

Colonel Kennedy staggered back as if shot. Never had he expected such a request. His face hardened, and he shot out, "Are you that determined to die?"

"I am determined, sir, to help those in need."

"Those men you seek to comfort tried to kill you yesterday."

"Colonel, they are still men."

Sighing heavily, the colonel sank into his chair, and his head bobbed ever so slightly. Richard forgot all about his aching muscles, even forgot to salute. He ran, dodging soldiers, horses, and cannon until he reached General Kershaw's headquarters. Only once he bolted through the front door, two lieutenants grabbed his arms.

"I need to see the general!" Richard demanded.

"General's busy, boy," one man shot back.

The other officer said softly, "You have to wait, son. If the general can spare a minute, maybe . . ."

Waiting proved as merciless as the begging. Richard anxiously watched men race up and down the staircase, scurrying around like ants. At the top of the stairs, General Kershaw barked orders. *Every minute that I wait,* Richard thought, *men are dying.*

When General Kershaw started down the stairs, Richard thought he had a chance. A lieutenant's stare, however, silently warned him to hold his tongue. Richard trembled. The general reached the floor, and turned toward the parlor.

"General!" he shouted. "Please!"

Immediately, the house fell silent. Richard felt certain he would be strung up by his thumbs as punishment. The general barely glanced at Richard before continuing, and Richard felt sick. His last hope . . . gone. Suddenly, General Kershaw stopped and turned.

"What is it, soldier?" he asked.

"General," Richard said, surprised to find his voice. "I want

175

to bring water to the wounded enemy."

"You'd be killed."

"Sir, I could wave a flag of truce."

"The enemy might think we're surrendering. I cannot allow that."

He realized the general hadn't said no, at least, not yet. "I'll do it without the white flag, sir, if you'll grant permission."

Seconds dragged on like hours as General Kershaw tugged his mustache. "It's a foolish request, but one so noble I cannot deny." He snapped a sharp salute. "I trust God will look after you."

Well, this is what I wanted, he thought once he had climbed over the wall and the first shots had barely missed him. Frigid air burned his lungs, and the canteens slung over Richard's shoulder felt like sacks of cannonballs. Another wail cut through the air, and Richard heard an enemy yell: "Kill him! It's a Rebel trick!"

Two more shots rang out, tearing the earth at his feet. His knees buckled, but he kept going, ignoring Denny's cries to hurry back. The fog had burned off by now, and he saw nothing but bodies and frozen blood.

"Water . . ."

Richard knelt. Now that he wasn't moving, the next shot would likely find its mark. Instead, a sudden silence greeted him. He lifted the soldier's head, and poured water into the mouth. Most of the liquid spilled down the gravely wounded man's cheeks, which Richard wiped with his bandanna. He stared at the face of his enemy, no older than Richard.

The boy swallowed, and his lips mouthed, "Thank you." Richard gave him another sip, then moved on.

The next man he reached was too weak to speak. The third was dead. Richard kept moving, always waiting for that bullet, but the weapons remained silent. For two hours, he went from enemy to enemy, bringing water and a moment of comfort until the last of his canteens was empty. As he gently eased a captain's head to the ground, he noticed the man shivering uncontrollably. Richard pulled off his greatcoat, and covered the man's body. "God bless you," the soldier said.

"God be with you," Richard replied, and headed back to the stone wall. All around him came a strange sound for a battlefield. Thousands of Union soldiers, men sworn to kill him, cheered and cheered and cheered. Confederates answered with their own hurrahs.

Before him, he saw Denny McBride's bright smile, and Richard no longer felt so cold.

THE BARBER OF FLORENCE

This wasn't the glorious war Teddy Sutter expected to find. Leaning against the siding of the rocking railroad car, he tried to fill his lungs with fresh air, which proved difficult. Crammed with hundreds of Union soldiers, the boxcar smelled of sweat and blood . . . even death.

It was September, but here in South Carolina it felt like the hottest summer day. Back home in Concord, fall would be showing its first colors. Papa would be at work, giving nickel shaves and ten-cent haircuts. And Mother? She had cried when Teddy and brother Matthew marched off to join the regiment. "He's only thirteen," Mother cried, holding Teddy tightly.

Teddy pleaded, though. "I've waited more than three years. If I don't go now, I'll never get to whip the Rebs."

Papa let them go. He wanted to join himself, but that wooden left leg prevented that. After telling Mother that her sons would be fighting to preserve the Union and free the slaves, he shook each boy's hand. Teddy tried to remember the scent of bay rum—Papa's hands always smelled like that after work—but foul air soiled his memory.

He didn't know what had happened to Matthew. One minute they were charging the Rebs, Teddy banging on his drum, trying to keep up as bullets whistled overhead, men screamed, and thick smoke filled the air. Then a shell exploded. Teddy woke up in the arms of Sergeant Timothy O'Rourke, who told him they were prisoners headed for Charleston.

Now, three months later, they were being moved again. To Florence, somebody said, wherever that was.

A shrill whistle cut through the air, the wheels screeched, and the train finally stopped. The doors soon slid open, and Teddy and his comrades stumbled outside, blinded by the sun. As his vision cleared, Teddy made out armed guards, many dressed in worn-out gray or pecan-colored uniforms, some in only homespun shirts and ragged britches. Few wore shoes.

"Twelfth New Hampshire!" Sergeant Timothy shouted hoarsely. "Fall in." The rail-thin Irishman smiled down at Teddy. "Let's go see our temporary home."

Home. In a field east of town, Teddy marched into a stockade made of pine logs about sixteen feet high. Much of the compound looked like a swamp; a small stream ran through the center of camp. Armed guards patrolled along platforms near the top of the log walls, and cannons rested on each corner. About twelve feet from the walls, a shallow trench had been dug.

"That's the deadline, Teddy," Sergeant Timothy said. "Don't cross that ditch or the Rebs will shoot you dead."

"Where do we sleep?" Teddy asked.

O'Rourke shrugged. "I reckon we'll have to build shelters ourselves."

Teddy, O'Rourke, and two other privates from the Twelfth, Ole Thorstad and James Grove, shared a small dugout covered with pine branches and Grove's coat. Each afternoon the prisoners were given a handful of flour, some cornmeal, two potatoes, and a small chunk of spoiling meat. They fell into a routine.

Sergeant Timothy became one of the prisoners' leaders. He approved the digging of tunnels and other plans, although few ever escaped. Hounds tracked down those who made it out.

Many prisoners often returned bloody and bruised, mauled by cruel dogs.

Thorstad served as cook for his bunkies. He filled his pot with water from the stream, put all of the food in it, and cooked it until the water boiled out. "Kush," he called it. It tasted awful, but Teddy was glad to have something in his stomach.

Grove scavenged around the camp, looking for anything that might come in handy. He had traded the buttons off his blue coat for Thorstad's cook pot.

Teddy wanted to do something, too, anything to earn his keep. "There's no drum for you to beat," Grove told him. "So what can you do?"

He thought for a minute and finally gave up, feeling worthless. He had no skill. He looked up sadly and saw Grove's long black hair. Suddenly, Teddy snapped his fingers. "I can cut your hair!"

After laughing briefly, Thorstad removed his cap and ran fingers through his locks. "Well, I could use a trim."

Sergeant Timothy smiled, too. "Private Grove, do you think you can find Private Sutter a pair of scissors?"

Teddy fashioned his shears using the broken blades of two folding jack knives, a piece of baling wire, and, for handles, three-inch pieces from a sweet gum branch. With his comb and makeshift scissors, he went to work. Sergeant Timothy was first, declaring afterward that he felt ten pounds lighter and ready to go dancing. Thorstad marveled how Teddy could do such a professional job, and Grove promised to pay two bits as soon as they got home.

Teddy swelled with pride. He wished Papa could see him now. Then he looked down, at the dirty rags that once had been his uniform, and took back that wish.

Word spread throughout the stockade of the young barber,

and Teddy became busy. He stood in front of the dugout while prisoners filed by to sit on a pine stump since there were no chairs. Teddy sheared away, sometimes trimming beards, always refusing payment. As soon as he almost felt happy, he saw a body being carried to the Dead House.

By November, the crowded stockade held 11,000 prisoners, many deathly sick. The stream turned into a cesspool, and the stench turned overpowering. O'Rourke developed a bad cough. Rebs cut the daily food supply to just cornmeal.

Around Christmas, a gaunt prisoner in miserable rags took his place on the pine stump. Lice-infested blond hair hung below the man's shoulders. Teddy swallowed and tried to comb the knotted hair. When the frail man began to weep, and his head dropped in shame, Teddy lowered his tools, almost broke into tears himself.

Yet something Papa often said in the barbershop flashed through his mind. "Hold your head up," Teddy said. He repeated the sentence softly. As if ordered by an officer, the feeble soldier stopped crying. Even straightened.

"Hold your head up," Teddy whispered. *You have nothing to be ashamed of,* he added silently. *Hold your head high.* Soon, Teddy spoke those words to every customer.

January passed into February. The weather turned cold, and late one morning Thorstad asked Teddy to stop working on a Massachusetts soldier's hair and come into the dugout. Teddy obeyed, slipping scissors and comb into his coat pocket, and knelt beside Sergeant Timothy.

The Irishman had been sick for a long time, but refused to go to the post hospital, saying every prisoner who went inside never came out, except feet first. O'Rourke weakly gripped Teddy's right hand.

"Laddie," he said in a faint voice. "Sorry you won't be able to cut my hair again." He coughed, but tried to smile.

Teddy's lips trembled.

"I'm proud of you," O'Rourke whispered. "Your folks will be, too. You've saved a lot of our boys here, helped them keep their spirits. Hold your head up, Teddy. I'll be in a better place." His eyes closed.

Thorstad and Grove removed their caps. "Go back to cutting hair," Thorstad said quietly. "He'd want you to, and the boys out there need you. We'll take care of Sarge."

Stumbling outside, feeling numb, Teddy walked to the pine stump. Slowly, he pulled out his scissors and comb. Through sobs, he managed to choke out words to his customer: "Hold your head up. Hold your head high."

Two days later, the Rebs ordered the prisoners to assemble. Rumors had drifted across the camp that Sherman's troops were pushing forward. Now a Rebel officer confirmed that rumor, telling the prisoners they would be shipped to North Carolina to be paroled. *Free.* The soldiers let out a deafening cheer. Teddy, though, couldn't smile, wishing Sergeant Timothy had lived to see this.

Teddy rode the train to Greensboro, clutching his makeshift scissors all the way. The war would soon be over. Of that, he was certain. The train pulled to a stop, and the ragged prisoners stepped onto the depot where, this time, Union soldiers stood waiting. Teddy stared at the clean men in spotless blue uniforms and shiny black leather. They looked back, aghast at the wretched condition of the prisoners.

Embarrassed, Thorstad fingered his grubby undershirt and studied his blackened bare feet. Grove trembled and looked away.

On the depot, an officer cleared his throat, struggled for

words. "We'll escort you . . . we'll . . . we'll get you cleaned up. Company, *attention.*"

Teddy examined his own ruined uniform, then saw the scissors. "Hold your head up," he said softly, first to himself, then to Thorstad and Grove. His words spread up the line.

"Hold your head up. Hold your head high."

Weakly, but with dignity, these soldiers, with their barber-drummer, marched past the line of men in blue, eyes front, heads high. They were soldiers of the United States of America. They had served her proudly. And they were going home.

WHEN I RODE WITH THE BOYS

Well, it's your call, I reckon. Same as it was mine twenty years back. Yeah, I rode to Lawrence all them years ago. I admit it. Don't regret most of what we done. It was a fine day of butchery. We Missourians had our reasons.

Frank James? His stepdad got strung up by the Yanks—didn't kill him, mind you, but they might have, and them bluecoats abused his brother, Jesse, who—don't believe what everybody in Kansas and practically the world swear as gospel—wasn't at Lawrence. Not that beautifully sunny August morning back in '63, nohow.

Cole Younger? Bluecoats or scum-sucking redlegs murdered his pa. Shot him down on a dirt road, then tossed his body in a ditch. And the Yanks never posted nobody for that killing, as cold-blooded as they come.

Bill Anderson? One of his sisters got killed when that prison collapsed in Kansas City. Drove poor Bill mad, 'cause he sure doted on Josephine. So did I. Yeah, I knowed Josephine. I . . . well . . . it's still hard to talk about her. Her death, you see, turned Bill into an animal, into Bloody Bill. Not that it took much doing, his mind being on the crazy side even before the war commenced.

Charley Hart? That's what we called William Quantrill, the Bloody Butcher of Lawrence, the Scourge of Kansas. He had his reasons, too. I just ain't exactly sure what they was. But me? Way I figure things, I had more reason to ride to Lawrence than

Frank or Cole or Billy or Charley or George Todd or Jim Cummins or Clell Miller or any of the boys. Mine was personal.

The handle they give me was Red Black. Red on account that my hair was like a carrot, or because, like Charley Hart once said, I was always seeing red, always wanting blood. Black because that was the color of my heart, after what happened in '63, and Black be my true last name. I told Charley Hart that my truthful name was Orrin Black, but that was a lie.

The name Ma and Pa saddled on me was Ophelia.

You see, I was—by jinks, still am—a woman.

Well, I wasn't much more than a girl in '63.

Folks still think of Lawrence as nothing short of murder, that we bushwhackers riding with devils like Quantrill and Anderson and Todd was mad-dog killers, and maybe we was. But we got drove to it. Since we turned out to be on the losing side of the War for Southern Independence, no one much listens to our side of the story. Nobody seems to recall that Kansas redlegs was mad-dog killers just like us Missouri folks, and that Senator Jim Lane of Kansas is likely burning in Hell as Lucifer's top lieutenant. Folks disremember what happened in Osceola, Missouri.

But I ain't.

Us Blacks didn't own no slaves, and Pa pretty much didn't care one whit about North or South. He tended his business as a wheelwright in Osceola. But my big brother, Lucas, well he was a regular fire-eater, him being old enough to recollect all the torment John Brown put this country through in the late '50s, and him seeing a much brighter future as a soldier finding glory in a by-god shooting war than following Pa's footsteps, sweating sunup to sundown over forges and lathes and reamers and chisels and big hoops of iron. So Lucas up and joined the Missouri State Guard, and he taken part in that little set-to at Wilson's Creek, but got disillusioned with all that marching and getting bossed around by sergeants and officers, so he quit for a spell, till he met Charley Hart and decided that he sure liked riding with the boys.

Before Charley Hart, however, come September 23, 1861, when Jim Lane's Jayhawkers rode into Osceola. They come calling with two cannon and hundreds of torches. Now if this was supposed to be an act of war, you explain why it was that the first place them Kansans stopped at was the bank. Taken the safe out, blowed it up, and when they found not much gold or silver, Lane himself went into a murderous rage. His men stormed into homes, taking money and china and silver, anything. They broke into businesses, taking everything they could. They stole hogs and chickens and horses and mules. A bunch of Jayhawkers decided to make war on the saloons and grog shops—most of them was so in their cups they had to be tossed into the back of wagons along with the plunder the other vermin had stole.

And Lane himself, acting as judge, jury, executioner, and God, brought out eight men to try for treason. When Pa stepped out and protested, they tossed him in with the other "defendants."

They shot all nine, left them lying dead in the streets, and then went to work with their torches.

That's why Lucas, my brother, found Charley Hart, and when the boys started avenging all the wrongs done upon us Missourians, when the black flag got raised, the war come to me, too.

Our boys didn't ask for no quarter, and they sure didn't give Yankees or redlegs none. Folks say armies are supposed to be civilized, that there be rules to what you can do and what you can't do in a time of war. Ask a Yank, and they'll tell you that everybody who rode with Quantrill or Bloody Bill was guilty of war crimes, deserved to be hanged or shot, but nobody ever

says much about Jim Lane or all them other redleg killers.
Nobody hardly even remembers what happened at Osceola.

So for the next year or more, things got hot in Missouri.
Charley Hart made things hot. Yanks would get ambushed, and
killed, and I reckon that when Charley and Lucas and the boys
ambushed some bluebellies in Westport on June 16, 1863, the
Yanks in charge decided they'd had enough. Fourteen bluebellies was killed in that fracas, so General Thomas Ewing Jr.
decided that us civilians—with kinfolk riding with the boys—
was just as guilty of war crimes as our soldier boys.

In July, some bluecoats rode up to home where I was tending
to Ma and my two younger sisters. Ma hadn't never much
recovered from the murder of Pa, so I had to do all the cooking
and cleaning and doctoring in the ashes and rubble that now
was Osceola, nothing more than a skeleton of what once had
been a right prosperous city.

A gray-bearded sergeant pounded on the rickety screen door
with the butt of his rifle, and I answered the door with a Colt's
Dragoon in my right hand and a scowl on my face.

"What you want?"

"Ophelia Black," he said.

"That's me."

Which is when I noticed about a half dozen other bluecoats
standing in the yard, with big muskets aimed at me.

"You can come with us alone," the sergeant said, "or we can
bring your mother and sisters with us, too."

"Where you taking me?"

"Kansas City."

"What for?"

"You're under arrest. For spying on the Union. For aiding
and abetting the murderous bushwhackers riding with William
Quantrill, alias Charley Hart."

Meaning helping my brother when he come home to see Ma.

Lucas had made himself famous after he'd lined up some blue-bellies who'd surrendered to see how many bodies a ball from a .58-caliber Enfield rifle would pass through.

My thumb scratched the hammer of the big .44.

"I've never popped a cap on a female," the sergeant said, "but you try something, and we won't just be burying you, young lady."

Well, I didn't have much choice, sure didn't want to see Ma and Julie and Naomi riding to Kansas City with me, to be put in chains and rot in prison. Nor could I stand to see them buried. So I talked the sergeant into letting me tell our neighbor what was going on, so Mr. and Mrs. Eager would look after my sisters and my ma. Then I rode north with the Yanks.

First time I'd ever seen Kansas City. First time I'd ever been out of Osceola. The big three-story brick structure was called the Thomas Building, located in the Metropolitan Block, known as McGee's Addition, on the east side of Grand Avenue between Fourteenth and Fifteenth. It was a right new building, and somebody told me a famous painter had been living in it for a spell, and had turned the third floor into his studio. I only got to see the second story, as that's what they had turned into the prison.

They was nine of us "spies" being held in the jail. Women. Girls, mostly, one not more than ten years old. Bill Anderson's sisters, Mary Ellen, Janie, and Josephine, was among them, Josephine being the middle one and at fourteen was my age, so we taken a liking to each other. Josephine helped me tend to Charity Kerr, who was sick in bed with a fever. Charity was one of Cole Younger's cousins. And there was McCorkles and Vandevers jailed, too. Them bluecoats had cut a wide swath hunting up us spies.

Well, before long Yanks on guard duty started moving some

support posts from the first floor, to give them more space. Another story I heard tell was that they was trying to tunnel to another jail cell where some strumpets was being imprisoned for indecency and prostitution. Most folks these days say what happened on August 13 was an accident. In 1863, we called it murder.

I was taking a wet rag off Charity Kerr's forehead, and was going to dip it in the bucket of water by the corner. The floor underneath me shifted, sending me sprawling. Come up cursing, brushing dust off me, I noticed dust sifting down from the ceiling.

"It done it again," Josephine said, coming to help me to my feet.

For a few days now, we had noticed the floor sagging, and Mrs. McCorkle had told the guards about it. One peachy-faced Yank even told us that the provost marshal had been informed and was to inspect the building that very day.

Well, I thanked Josephine and I cursed the Yanks as fools and went to find the bucket, while Josephine returned to Charity.

Then it happened. The floor just fell out from under me, and I was screaming, only I couldn't hear them screams because of the roar of bricks and timber falling all around me. Then I couldn't hardly say nothing because the dust was so thick, choking, and my left arm was just burning in pain, and I was blind, and crying, and screaming, and praying, and cursing—all at the same time.

Here's where things happened, and it taken me a while for me to sort out. No, I ain't rightly sure I ever got it all sorted out. What I saw, when the dust cleared, was Josephine Anderson kneeling over me.

"My arm!" I cried. "I can't move it." I wailed and blubbered—shames me to admit it—but I was fearing my life. Couldn't hardly see nothing but dust and bricks all around me, and I just knowed I was going to be buried alive.

"Hush!" Josephine snapped, and she managed to get them bricks off my arm. She eased me up, dragged me away just before another wall of bricks crashed down. Would've buried me alive. "Go on," she said, pointing. "I'll find Charity."

Holding my busted limb gingerly, I picked my way through the rubble, and happened upon Mrs. McCorkle—she allowed that she was living only because she jumped out of a window when the walls started to fall.

Mrs. McCorkle steered me to the streets, where folks was standing, gawking. I turned, and choked out Josephine's name, and looked, but by then the dust and rubble had swallowed her. I saw nothing but Yankee guards running through the ruins of the Thomas Building. Somebody taken me from Mrs. Mc-Corkle, and led me toward Fifteenth, even put my busted limb in a sling fashioned out of a scarf. He wasn't no Yankee, if my memory's straight, just a civilian. He also give me a handkerchief, which I used to wipe away the cuts and grime covering my face.

Civilians started to enter the Hades to help bring our women out. I just stood, as policemen and firemen arrived to help. Suddenly, I spied two Yankees hauling a busted-up woman in a blue calico dress out of the ruins. A man in a sack suit and carrying a satchel run up to them just as the bluecoats just dropped the woman on the ground like a sack of wheat.

"Don't mess with her, Doc," one of the bluecoats told the man with the satchel. "She's dead."

I had started back toward the mounds of bricks, but the Yankee's words stopped me. I blinked, shaken my head, and looked harder. There wasn't no mistaking that blue calico dress, or that girl's hair. That was Josephine Anderson.

Lying there.

Dead.

She who'd just saved my life.

A horse whinnied behind me, and I turned. Some fool had dismounted to help the wounded and the dead, leaving this buckskin mare on Grand Avenue. Bluecoats wasn't paying no attention to me. Nobody was, so I managed to climb into that saddle, busted arm tormenting me something fierce, and rode out of Kansas City.

Folks ask me nowadays how I done it, but it wasn't so hard. A farmer on the Blue helped splint up my busted arm, and he give me some boys' duds to wear. He didn't know what I had in mind, just knowed that I was bad hurt and he was loyal to the gray. He didn't see me take the strips of cotton, which I somehow managed to wrap around my chest and conceal them breasts. Which wasn't hard as I was never blessed with ample cleavage like that naked lady yonder over the back bar in this here bucket of blood.

There had been a Navy Colt in the saddlebags of the horse I liberated, and after I left the farmer's cabin, I stuck it in my waistband.

I rode in the dark, and happened upon some other boys who was wearing the embroidered shirts of bushwhackers; I was wearing an oversized shirt of dirty muslin. They taken me for a Yankee, but I told them: "I'm looking for Lucas Black. My brother. He rides with Charley Hart."

"He did," Frank James answered. "Till Yanks killed him at the Junction in Wyandotte County a few weeks back."

Like some weak petticoat, I toppled off my horse in a dead faint.

They taken me to Perdee's, where Charley Hart had ordered the boys to meet up, where he would plan retaliation for the murder of those sisters of the Confederacy, killed in Kansas City.

191

"Who are you?" Charley Hart asked.

"I'm Orrin Black," I told him. "Lucas was my brother."

He wet his lips, thin they was, hardly no color to them. "He never mentioned a brother to me."

"He never mentioned you to me."

Which got them thin lips turning upward in a grin. "How'd you bust your arm, Red Black?"

"I was in that Kansas City jail," I said. No lie there. "They didn't just keep women there."

So I told them everything that I could remember. All that dirt and mortar I'd swallowed had deepened my voice, so I reckon I sounded like a man, or, at the least, a boy, and my face was scratched and bruised and filthy. My dirty hair was long, but so was the hair of most of the boys. Jim Cummins later told me he'd get his locks shorn after he'd killed two hundred bluecoats, and not before.

When I was done talking, Charley Hart said, "I ride to Lawrence."

There was some, but not much, debate, maybe because I'd told the boys how the Yanks had moved those timbers, how that had likely caused the bricks to fall and bury our women, how it was murder, plain and simple.

Bloody Bill Anderson, sobbing over the death of his kid sister, cried out, "It is Lawrence or Hell. And we kill every male in that Yankee cesspool, and leave it in ashes."

"Remember Osceola!"

We rode out at daybreak. By the time we stood in our stirrups southeast of Lawrence, there was four hundred of us. We galloped into that Yankee city, home of Jim Lane and other redleg butchers, with no flag, just revolvers in our hands and murder in our hearts.

So, after all these years, what is there to say?

That we killed our first man, a minister, while he sat on a stool milking his cow?

That we burned and looted as vilely as Jim Lane's men had done in Osceola?

That Bill Anderson made his victims crawl to him on their hands and knees, look up at him and beg for their lives before he shot them dead? "I am here for revenge!" he yelled, tears streaming into his own dark beard.

That we left the town a smoldering ruin, with nigh two hundred folks to bury?

That I watched this without remorse? That I killed men and boys myself?

Smoke blackened the morning sky, but above the roaring of flames, the breaking of glass, and the pops of pistols rose the deafening—to me, at least—wails of the people of Lawrence.

I was standing with Cole Younger and Frank James in front of a house that several other bushwhackers was finishing looting and setting afire.

"You hungry?" Frank asked.

"I could eat," Cole answered.

Cole pointed to a three-story home across the street. "Boys," he said, "that house is protected. Don't burn it. Don't kill anyone there."

"At least," Frank said, as he reloaded one of his Remington revolvers, "till after we've taken our breakfast."

When someone chuckled, Cole whirled. "I'm serious. That place is protected."

I didn't even glance at Cole or Frank or none of the boys. I stared at the man lying on the steps of the house we was pillaging, his life's blood staining the whitewashed steps, and the man's young wife—now widow—kneeling over his body, sobbing.

"Let's go," Frank said, and he led the boys across the street.

I did not go. I meant to. But the widow looked up at me, and she had removed the butcher's knife from her dead husband's chest. Before I could do anything, she plunged the knife into her own heart.

We always claimed that we killed only men and boys in the Lawrence raid. Maybe we did. But I'd have to say we had a hand in that woman's death.

I turned, started to follow Cole and Frank, but then I heard something above all that misery. From inside that house, a baby cried.

So I ran inside the burning home.

It was a boy. Just a baby. I brung him out of the fire, and found a rocking chair someone had left behind. I sat there, rocking the baby till he fell asleep in my arms. Then, staring at the sleeping child, so peaceful among all this horror, I remembered something. It come to me clear.

I am being helped out of the bricks and ruins of the Kansas City jail, but it is not Josephine Anderson saving me. It couldn't have been. The wall of bricks had crushed Josephine, who had died near Charity Kerr. A Yankee pulls me out of that ruin. A Yankee saves my life.

I sat rocking the baby and cried. Our boys rode by, but few paid attention to me. Why should they? Like most of the city, that house had become an inferno. There were other places to loot, and they had to hurry before Yankee troops come seeking their own revenge.

Cole and Frank and a handful of others left the house across the street. True to their word, they did not burn that building or harm its occupants, who fled as soon as the bushwhackers had gone, to hide in the cornfields. Leaving that house for me and the baby I held.

Bloody Bill Anderson would kill fourteen people himself in

Lawrence, but his thirst for vengeance would never be slaked. He would die himself. So would Charley Hart. The boys rode out of Lawrence, but they rode without me. I don't know if they even missed me. Probably figured I was drunk like that one fool that stayed behind and got shot to pieces when the Yankees did arrive.

That evening, bluecoats and Lawrence survivors found not Red Black, but a young girl in her teens, sitting on the front porch of one of the few homes not burned by the bushwhackers, letting a baby boy suckle on a bottle of milk. The dress I wore did not fit well, but folks—Yankees never being the smartest in the world—figured I'd busted my arm during the raid, and those bruises on my face, the filthy red hair, my rugged appearance was nothing out of the norm on that terrible evening of August 21, 1863.

"That's Matthew and Lois's baby!" someone said, and this middle-aged woman still in her nightshirt came up on the porch.

I nodded, as if I knew.

Jim Lane had come out of the cornfield, where he had hidden like the miserable coward he was, during the entire raid. Others no longer hid. Most were in shock.

I pushed myself out of the rocking chair, and handed the baby to the woman.

"You poor thing," the lady said. "You poor, poor thing." Maybe she was talking to the baby. Maybe to me. I didn't know. Didn't care.

I walked right past Jim Lane, who nodded at me. I didn't nod back, but I didn't kill him, neither. I had seen too many people die.

Getting out of Lawrence was as easy as getting out of Kansas City after the jail collapsed. I found a mule, not even worth stealing, crossed the ferry, and just drifted back to Missouri.

Yanks crisscrossed the country for Charley Hart and his bushwhackers, but nobody cared much about some teenaged girl with a bum left limb riding a mule blind in one eye.

So I come home to Osceola. To bury Ma eight months later after General Ewing's General Order No. 11 kicked all families of bushwhackers out of western Missouri. My sisters wound up in an orphanage, and I went to work in St. Joe.

Eventually, the war ended, more or less. Jim Lane killed himself. Some bushwhackers kept the fight going by robbing banks and trains. Cole Younger got shot to pieces in Minnesota robbing a bank and is up there today in prison with his brothers. Frank's awaiting trial over in Gallatin, having surrendered after his brother, Jesse, got killed here in St. Joe by that coward Bob Ford. And I just run this saloon.

So here you are. Don't know how you found me, but I'm glad you did. Matthew, eh? Named you after your pa. Them neighbors who adopted you brung you up good. Strapping you are. No, I can't tell you nothing about your ma or your pa, because I didn't know them. I just saw them die twenty years back. Same as I saw my own ma and pa die. Same as I saw Josephine Anderson die. Same as I saw far too many people die.

Yeah, I reckon I saved your life, fetching you from that burning house in Lawrence, but I rode with the boys, and I sure ain't no hero. I killed at least two of your neighbors. And I done nothing to prevent your ma's and your pa's deaths. Riding with the boys? That was my call. At the time, I thought it was the right one.

If you've come to kill me, to get your own revenge, well, that's your right. If you want another shot of rye, I can accommodate you there, too. Like I say, it's your call.

★ ★ ★ ★ ★

COWBOY STORIES

★ ★ ★ ★ ★

After four horse wrecks, two cracked ribs, and other injuries, I have learned that writing about cowboys is a lot easier than trying to be one . . .

THE SNORING MAN

I knew Vince Caliente would be nothing but trouble the day he walked into the bunkhouse in 1886. Hell, I couldn't even pronounce his name. What I should have done was packed my possibles in my war bag and lit a shuck for Tascosa, but the winter was shaping to be one of the worst to hit the Panhandle and I didn't fancy freezing to death on the banks of the Canadian. So I, Lucas Jackson Hardee, made one big mistake. I stayed.

Caliente was a big man, standing about six-foot-five and weighing more than a longhorn bull. He went through horses about as fast as he went through a plate of beans. And ornery? He could whip a grizzly with his bare hands, but instead of beating up on bears, which were right scarce in the Panhandle, he liked to tear the lungs out of cowhands, which were plentiful on the Lazy M. The way he seen it, there weren't nothing better after a good meal than a shot of whiskey or an old-fashioned fisticuff. And seeing that foreman Artie Moreno didn't allow whiskey on the spread except for doctoring, and the nearest settlement was a day's ride from the Lazy M, Caliente tackled the other cowhands on the ranch.

No one liked Caliente, and I ain't never figured out why Moreno hired him. He couldn't rope, ride, keep his saddle clean, or do any of the easy chores around the ranch. And on top of all that, the son of a bitch snored.

I reckon the snoring was the sixth round in the chamber,

because Caliente's snoring wasn't like that of any other cowhand. It was like a sick Hereford moaning: loud, erratic, and irritating. And by Christmastime, I was on edge worst than a greenhorn mounting a wild mustang. And so was Sourdough Frankie, Earl McCarty, Charly Reno, Dan Jernigan, and Henri Ombrageux. It seemed Vince Caliente was the only cowboy on the Lazy M that winter who was getting any rest.

That's what started it all.

The first few nights, we had just tolerated it, figuring we would get used to it. But Caliente's snoring got louder and louder, and the rest of us were getting tireder with each sunrise. And winter weren't no picnic in the Texas Panhandle. We had to keep us and a passel of Lazy M beeves from freezing, and six trees didn't do much good as a windbreak. It didn't take long for a man to die of exposure during a blizzard neither. I had buried my share of frozen cowboys.

We had tried everything, from putting pillows over our heads to trying to get to sleep before Caliente, but none of it done no good. The pillows was like trying to muffle a stampede, and I never could fall right asleep—I rolled over more than a hog in the summer. But Caliente would waddle to his bunk and be sawing before I had time to cuss. And all of us was light sleepers, so even if we did happen to nod off first, Caliente's snores would wake us up and send us tossing and cussing like we was riding an outlaw mustang.

One night we even tried to roll Caliente over because Henri had read that that was a cure for snoring. But that worked as well as Custer's plan on the Big Horn. We got Caliente turned over all right, but Henri, who was as thin as a strand of barbed wire, almost got trampled to death by that bull, before Caliente woked up and sent me sleeping with one less tooth.

And then hell broke loose on Christmas week.

Artie Moreno came in while we was eating breakfast after

another night of little sleep. "I ain't never seen such a sorrier looking bunch in all my days," he said. "Vince is the only one who looks fit." We grumbled some, and Moreno continued. "There's a norther moving in, and I want to move those cattle on the East Range over to the Big Blue where the grass is a little better. Ain't no way they can survive where they're at if we get much more snow." He paused for a minute, looking us over, then said, "Vince, I want you to take Lucas, Dan, and Charly and move those head today. You're in charge."

Dropping his fork in his plate, Jernigan looked up, not pleased with the chain of command. "I been here five years, know that land better than anybody, 'cept for Earl. I ought to be in charge."

"Ordinarily, you would be," Moreno said. "But Dan, you don't look worth a buffalo bone, and I want Earl to check the fence along Stoney Creek. You could use some sleep."

I knowed it would be a long day and dreaded it. Caliente was bad enough to work with, but he was impossible to work for. Caliente swore he would shoot anyone he found asleep and rode us harder than we drove the cattle. The saddle bum put Jernigan at drag, and Dan Jernigan was the best point man I ever worked with. Drag was the spot for tenderfeet or slow, fat tramps like Caliente, but the big man took point.

We made it back around suppertime. I don't know what McCarty and Henri had talked about while we was gone, but Henri walked up to Caliente while we was eating and said, "Vince, we've got a little problem."

Caliente finished slopping up his beans and looked up, ornery as ever. "State yer business."

"Vince, your snoring has been keeping us awake. Now, I don't know what you can do about it, but—"

Caliente's right fist caught the little Frenchman square in the jaw and sent him reeling toward the wall. McCarty jumped up and took hold of the big man's arms, and Charly, Jernigan, and

I went to help. Between the four of us, I figured, we could take him. I found out just how wrong I was in a minute. Caliente broke McCarty's grip, kicked Jernigan in his privates, and decked Charly with a left uppercut. The big man moved quick. I got the only punch in, but it didn't bother him. Ignoring me, he turned and gave McCarty a savage head slap, then hit him in the nose. By the time he turned around, I had raised a chair, but I never was that good a fighter, too slow. Caliente hit me in the stomach and I almost coughed up Frankie's beans. I dropped the chair, and he brought both of his fists down on my neck, and I joined Jernigan, Charly, and McCarty on the floor.

By then, Henri was getting to his feet. The rest of us was out of it. We hadn't had enough sleep to put up a struggle, and Caliente walked over to Henri and started beating the little man senselessly. If Sourdough Frankie hadn't pulled out his old Parker shotgun, Caliente might would have killed him.

"Hold it, Vince," Frankie warned, cocking both barrels. "Put the little man down, or I'll put you down."

A sawed-off scattergun can persuade most anybody, even a 300-pound, two-legged bull bastard.

But beating up Henri was the biggest mistake Vince Caliente would ever make. We all liked the little man, so did everybody around the Canadian. Henri couldn't move his neck, and it was obvious he had some busted ribs and a broken jaw. Artie Moreno and Sourdough Frankie decided to take the Frenchman into Tascosa the next morning. That was Moreno's biggest mistake. By leaving the Lazy M, he sealed Caliente's fate.

That night Jernigan brought in a full bottle of whiskey he had bought that fall from a peddler near the Indian Nations. Caliente was eating supper with the rest of us, complaining about my cooking. Setting the bottle in front of the big man, Jernigan said, "Here, Vince. I reckon Moreno was right about you being in charge the other day. I'm still upset at you for beating up

Henri like you did, but this is to show you no hard feelings."

Caliente looked up. "Ya worthless Yank," he said. "Yer tryin' to poison me. Well, yer gonna drink this whiskey and ya ain't gonna spill a drop."

"No, Vince," Jernigan pleaded. "You got it all wrong. This whiskey ain't bad. I was just saving it for a special occasion. Besides, it's Christmas Eve."

Caliente replied by cocking his rusty Walker Colt, which none of us knowed if it would fire or not but none of us was willing to find out.

So we had to pass the bottle around, each of us taking a small swig. If Moreno had found out we had whiskey in the bunkhouse, he would have fired us. Jernigan was fixing to take his second swig when Caliente grabbed the bottle and started guzzling. "Merry Christmas, boys," he said and laughed. The fat hog waddled to his bunk, drank the whiskey, and passed out about an hour later. I should have knowed he would snore even louder drunk.

We got up around midnight and dressed. "You sure you wanna go through with this?" I asked, feeling uneasy. No one answered. Charly and me took hold of the feet of Caliente's bunk, while McCarty and Jernigan grabbed the head of the bed.

"If he wakes up, he's gonna kill us all," I warned.

"He ain't gonna wake up," McCarty said nervously. "Not after all that whiskey he drunk. Shame we had to waste it on him."

Jernigan sighed, but perked up when Charly said, "It don't matter. I got a bottle of some good rye in my war bag. Been savin' it for a special occasion."

We lifted the bunk, but it weren't easy. Slowly, straining, we inched our way to the bunkhouse door. It took us a good 10 to 15 minutes, but we made it and lowered the bunk to the floor. I opened the door, and the north wind whipped in, howling like mad but not drowning out Caliente's snores. It was bitter cold outside, and I was glad to get back beside the stove after we had left Caliente in his bunk outside. Providing he stayed asleep, we had it made. But I still felt sick.

"They'll hang us if they ever find out," I said.

"He shouldn't've beaten up old Henri," Jernigan said. "And they ain't gonna find out. Get some sleep."

I didn't have to put up with Caliente's snoring, but I couldn't sleep. Neither could nobody else. We just waited in our bunks, listening to the wind bay. We got up hours later and moved Caliente inside. Except for the wind, the bunkhouse was quiet, like a funeral parlor, but none of us slept that night.

We were lucky we hadn't waited to do our deed because Artie Moreno came back the next morning. He said the way the storm was moving in, he didn't want to get snowed in at Tascosa, so he sent Henri and Sourdough Frankie ahead. Then we told him about Caliente, about how it seemed he died in his sleep. Moreno frowned and went to look at the big man's corpse, stiff as a fence post in his bunk. He came out, still frowning, and looked at us with a hanging judge's eyes. "What happened?"

McCarty shook his head. "We ain't figured it out, Mr. Moreno. He took hold of a bottle last night, downed it, and passed out in his bunk. Just never did wake up."

"Might could have swallowed his tongue," Jernigan offered.

"Yeah," Moreno said. "It looks to me like he froze to death. You sure he stayed in his bunk all night?" He wasn't believing a word. Moreno looked at me. "Lucas," he said. "I know you wouldn't lie. What happened?"

Shaking my head, I swallowed and replied, "I didn't hear Caliente get out of his bunk."

Moreno didn't buy it, but after what Caliente did to Henri, I don't think he cared too much for the tramp. He shook his head, told us to bury him, and started for the door, then hesitated and turned around. "I know it's bad, losing a fellow hand, but it is Christmas. Drop by the main house after supper tonight and we'll have a couple of drinks. It's going to be a long winter." He turned and left.

My stomach was a little queasy about what we had done. I mean, there weren't no other word for it but cold-blooded murder. I felt a lot better, however, after I ate a big supper, had a couple of drinks, and got a good night's sleep.

THE TIME WE BURIED CALEB KETCHUM

That was a hot, dry summer when Caleb Ketchum got rubbed out, throwed from his horse into a boulder that broke his neck. Ain't the best way for a cowhand to go to his reward—that's dying under the hoofs in a stampede—but this way there was enough left of him to bury good and proper.

Which is what we decided to do.

The Methodists was holding their July dance when we rode into town in our Sunday-go-to-meetings, and the Methodists didn't mind us Diamond J boys dropping by to shake a leg, but we was in town on somber business. To bury one of the best. March him down Front Street all the way to the graveyard—and not Boot Hill, neither, but the regular cemetery—and give him a Christian planting. Old Caleb deserved more than a canvas tarp, empty prairie, and a couple words read over him by a ramrod.

Lije Tolbert and Sean MacGregor had took Caleb to Olgethorpe the undertaker after he got killed, so we went there to pick him up in his fine pine coffin. Olgethorpe said we could've rented his hearse, but we didn't see no need in splurging. We'd just walk him to the cemetery. The Baptist preacher, Tidball, was to be waiting for us there along with two mourners Olgethorpe provided hisself.

So with Lije and MacGregor at the point, me and Luke Christie at flanks, and Hernandez and Jingle Bob Benteen pulling drag, we walked Caleb's coffin out of Olgethorpe's, into the center of Front Street, kicking up dust like we was pushing cattle, moving past Higginbotham's Tonsorial Parlor and Bell's Gun Shop, away from the Methodists, and toward the final resting place of many a good man.

But damn was it hot.

Texas sun ain't like no ordinary sun—and I've cowboyed from the Nueces to the Powder, so I know. Ordinary sun'll just make you sweat, grow tired, and feel miserable all day, then give you the night to recuperate. Texas sun, though, she'll beat you into the ground all day, like a heavy sledgehammer pounding a railroad spike, then pretend to be the moon and make you sweat half the night.

And us in our heavy black broadcloth and woolens! Come about the time we passed Youngman's Mercantile we was wishing we had taken Olgethorpe up on his offer of a hearse. Least, I was. Cowboys ain't much use afoot, and we had a ways to go. When we got to Amos Hardings's Saloon and Gambling Parlor, Lije called for us to whoa and looked toward them batwing doors.

"Boys," Lije finally said, "I do believe ol' Caleb would want to join us for a round before we sent him off to Perdition."

So, despite Amos Hardings's protests, we walked into the saloon and set Caleb down in his pine coffin on a poker table, then pulled up chairs around him. Amos was hollering at us to get out, that he liked Caleb well enough but he weren't serving no dead cowhand, but Luke Christie shut him up by throwing a wad of Yankee greenbacks at him. Hell, there weren't nobody else in there—all the sinners was with the Methodists—so Amos picked up the money and brought us glasses and a couple bottles of whiskey.

"To the Diamond J," Hernandez said, and we all raised our glasses, then downed our drinks. Funny how bad whiskey can burn your throat like the gates of Hell, but still cool you off on a hot day.

Another shot of whiskeys and MacGregor said, "Just like an Irish wake."

"Caleb, he weren't no Irishman was he?" Jingle Bob asked.

That got me to laughing. Caleb Ketchum didn't have much use for the Irish. Didn't have much use for nobody really unless they was Texicans. I shared my thoughts with the boys, and that got Lije to howling and hooting so much he could hardly breathe. He finally managed, "Damnedest thing to that is Caleb weren't no Texican."

We was all taken aback, but Lije, he knowed Caleb better than anyone. "Caleb was from Cassville, Georgia, just like me." Lije laughed some more. "Said he'd kill me if I ever told anyone." Lije tapped his shot glass on the coffin. "Sorry, Caleb."

Jingle Bob started pounding his fists on the table. "That's it!" he yelled. "That's it! All of us'll take turns telling a story about ol' Caleb. True story. Just like a preacher might." Jingle Bob was standing up then, that whiskey gone straight to his head. "Bartender!" he bellowed. "I do believe we're gonna need at least one more bottle."

Well, we all thought a mite and drank a bit, no one wanting to go first. Finally, MacGregor cleared his throat and said, "Well, now, I remember once—" and then he was looking at Christie, telling him, "now I hope you don't get too mad about this, Luke, but Caleb made me swear never to tell you." Christie just smiled and MacGregor stood up.

"Ol' Caleb," MacGregor said and he stopped to rest his hand fondly on the coffin lid. "He never really cared much about Luke's luck with the cards. Luke could sit down at a crooked table at Fort Griffin and walk away with a gambler's silk shirt. Caleb, he could sit down with them Methodists and lose his saddle." That got a few hoots, even one from Amos, who was cleaning glasses behind the bar. "So me and him and Luke was in the bunkhouse once and Luke stepped away to the privy, and Caleb he just stacked the deck and pretended to shuffle, asked me to cut—course, he had told me what he was doing and told me to decline the cut, or else—so I did and promptly folded. Luke had a full house and Caleb had a straight flush. Musta took you for half-a-month's wages."

MacGregor sat down as we laughed, and Christie pushed his hat back a bit and stared at the coffin. "I remember that," he said softly. "You sorry old bastard." That got us to laughing more.

Well, I figured I might as well go next. Most folks knowed my tale, but a good story can go a long ways in Texas. Bad story, too. "Y'all know Gwen Parsons?" I said, stumbling as I found my feet after all them whiskeys. Jingle Bob knowed what was coming and almost split his britches he was laughing so hard.

"It was right before the Methodists' Christmas dance about two years back, and me and Caleb had to ride to town to pick up some supplies. And there she was, staring through the window at Youngman's, just as perty as can be."

Everybody nodded 'cause they knowed how perty Gwen Parsons can be.

"Well, Caleb he started riding me to go over and ask her to the dance. Now, I wanted to take her—y'all know I could fancy that woman—but I sure didn't have the nerve to ask." I took a deep breath and had another whiskey. "But Caleb convinced me, so I walked up to her with hat in hand, exchanged some pleasantries, and asked her right there in front of Jory Peterson of the Double Seven. And she smiles and says to me, 'Why, I'd love to go with you, but Caleb has already asked me.'"

I had to sit down in a hurry—always do when I tell that story, it's just awful painful—and them boys was laughing up a storm, so I poured myself another whiskey. Jingle Bob bellowed, "Ol' Caleb, he never forgot that. He said you looked like a stuck pig when she told you that."

"Set you up, he did," MacGregor said. "He truly could be a bastard."

"Oh, I wanted to kill him," I said, and forced a smile.

Jingle Bob was still laughing. "Well, Caleb sure was a lady's man, that's the Lord's truth," he said.

"I don't know about all that," Hernandez softly said. "My cousin Teresa said her neighbor Juanita went out with Caleb once, but came home crying and didn't stop crying for days."

"Caleb didn't have much use for Mexicans either," I said.

"Well," Lije said, "he had one use for 'em."

We were silent for a minute, then Christie said to me, "Calhoun, I can tell you Gwen wasn't too happy at that Christmas dance. I cut the rug with her and she said she wasn't having that swell a time."

More laughter, more drinks, then Lije said kinda somber-like, "Hell, that's just like him. Reason he had to leave Cassville was 'cause he got the preacher's daughter in the family way. Preacher's daughter, mind you! Lit a shuck out of town one night at a high lope so he wouldn't have to marry the gal. Nice gal, too."

"Preacher's daughter!" Jingle Bob said and burst into laughter, beating his fists again on the table before stopping suddenly.

He was the only one laughing.

"Ever loan Caleb any money?" Hernandez asked no one in particular.

"Oh gosh," Lije said, rocking his chair on the rear legs, shaking his head slowly. "Who ain't?"

"Ever get any of it back?"

That got a cackle from Christie, who slowly filled his glass.

"He was a skinflint, that's for certain." He took a sip, shook his head, and said, "Remember back when Al Wilson died under the hoofs trying to turn that stampede in Kansas?" Lije, Mac-Gregor, and I nodded, but that was before the others joined the Diamond J.

"Good hand, Wilson," Lije said.

"Left behind a fine woman and passel of kids," I said.

Christie nodded. "And we passed the hat in Dodge City to take back to 'em. I bet I collected from ever' hide hunter, cowhand, just about ever' body in Dodge. But not Caleb, no-sireebob." Christie paused long enough to finish his whiskey. "Told me no way in hell he was giving away his hard-earned money."

"Hell," I said, "he probably started the stampede in the first place."

"He sure as hell didn't try to turn the herd," MacGregor said. "But Al Wilson did, by God!"

"*To Al Wilson!*" I yelled, and we all raised our glasses and downed whiskeys.

"Whoa, this herd is straying," Jingle Bob said, slurring his words. "Now, I'll be the first to admit Caleb had his faults—shoot, he almost killed me when he put that burr under my saddle back in April—but he was a Diamond J hand."

"Amen," Lije said.

"And the Diamond J is the best!"

We all "amened" and "damn righted" and poured ourselves more whiskeys while Jingle Bob preached up some fire and brimstone. "And Caleb Ketchum was the best!"

You could hear the squeaking of glasses from the bar as Amos wiped them with his rag, but that was about it. We thought for a minute, long and hard, had another round, and thought some more.

"Musta been some good deed that sumbitch did in his life,"

Christie said.

"Left Cassville, Georgia," Lije said. "Folks there probably think that was the best thing ever happened to them."

Bottles and glasses empty, we all started staring at the coffin on the table, listening to the music from the Methodists, a dog bark somewhere down the street. Nice, quiet summer day.

"Wonder if that preacher is still waiting for us at the graveyard?" Lije said softly, but nobody answered. MacGregor tugged on his mustaches a bit, then said, "Perty music."

Me, I couldn't help myself. "Wonder if Gwen's there?"

And suddenly, all six of us was looking at each other, smiling.

I reckon I should have titled this account something different 'cause we never got around to burying Caleb Ketchum. We just left him on the poker table at Amos Hardings's Saloon and Gambling Parlor and moseyed on down toward the Methodists.

"Hey!" Amos hollered from the front of his saloon. "Don't you leave Ketchum's coffin in here. You boys get back here! What the hell am I supposed to do with that damned thing?"

Lije laughed and said, "He's your friend. Bury him."

That got us all to cackling as Amos cussed up a storm. Last words we could savvy was: "He weren't no friend of mine. Son of a bitch owed me twenty dollars!"

RED RIVER CROSSING

If you've ever met Abel Head Pierce, you know he's a hard man, and not always fair-minded. Honest, certainly, but I've never known him to own up to a mistake, and I have known him for forty-odd years. The closest he ever came to apologizing, or admitting that he was wrong, started with an incident that happened back in 1871; and then, it wasn't until 1884 that Mr. Pierce hinted, in his own peculiar way, that he might have been a shade off being right during his dealings with Tom Griffin. I should know. I saw it all, at Red River Crossing, and later in Kansas, Texas, Arkansas, up the Texas Cattle Trail, and, finally, thirteen years later, in Dodge City.

Folks call him Shanghai, and he strutted like a Shanghai rooster when I first met him in '55 during a trail drive to Louisiana. He sounded like one, too, the way he cussed in a high-pitched voice that pricked your skin worse than fingernails scraping a chalkboard. Mr. Pierce stood six-foot-four in his stocking feet, hailed from Rhode Island, but made his mark in Texas cattle.

In the years I had ridden for Mr. Pierce since that first drive to Louisiana, his wealth and power had grown. Down in Texas, and practically all over the West, Abel Head Pierce had a hard-rock reputation as an almighty shrewd businessman and a top-rate cattleman. By the spring of 1871, he was a thirty-seven-year-old rancher, ramrod, and rapscallion, and he loved every minute of it when things were going his way. At Red River

Crossing, things didn't go his way, and he blamed Tom Griffin.

Let me concede that he was absolutely right in doing so. At first, I mean. Tom Griffin accepted the blame for what happened. Tom Griffin, you see, could admit his own mistakes, but this one proved costly.

It came during the height of the long drives from South Texas to Kansas. The Red River was flooding—highest I've ever seen it—and I warrant there had to be 60,000 cattle waiting to cross. Mr. Pierce realized the trouble, the danger, as we had three herds of 2,000 each with too many neighbors. So we invited each trail boss to our camp for son-of-a-bitch stew and Sourdough Frankie's fine biscuits and strong coffee. After supper, Mr. Pierce gave his instructions.

"It's been a wet one, boys," he said, "and my steers have done so much swimming, they look more like sea lions than longhorns." Of course, Mr. Pierce added a handful of salty expressions to that statement, words that a Methodist would frown upon but a cowboy would surely enjoy. Then he turned serious.

"I'm not one who takes unnecessary risks when it comes to my cattle and my money. We need to separate these herds, so I'm asking you to back off ten or twelve miles each. Wait for the water to fall, then we can cross in good order. Problem with the way our herds are bunched together, if one stampedes, it'll play hell on all of us."

That coaxing might have worked, too, if not for Tom Griffin. A strong-willed Texian, Griffin had survived the War of the Rebellion and a string of lousy luck. That spring, he had his hands full fending off carpetbaggers with designs on taking his ranch from him.

"I suppose you'll be crossing first, Shanghai?" he said.

"Nope. Them Mexicans from Refugio County got here first."

"Well, I just don't see it, Shanghai," Griffin said. "There are so many cattle here if each of us backs up ten miles or so, hell, I'd be back where I started from, and I, for one, don't aim at missing the market in Abilene."

Move back, and they feared they'd lose their turn crossing the river, and every man jack of them wanted to get to the Kansas railhead first, when the buyers had plenty of money to throw around. "Hell," Griffin argued, "nothing is going to happen."

So they stayed put, and three–four days later, one of the herds spooked. A match, snapping twig, coyote, who knows what started it? But it happened. It didn't take much, and that stampede spread like a prairie fire. Another herd ran. And another. Every herd camped near the banks of the Red spooked. It proved to be one of biggest disasters and damnedest sights I ever saw. Mr. Pierce had been right, Tom Griffin wrong, and there would be hell to pay.

I could hear Mr. Pierce's curses from camp as I rode in that night with a couple of the boys and the body of Blue Ben draped in my sugans and tied behind the cantle of Clete Jarnigan's zebra dun. Reports were already coming in of dead cattle, busted-up wagons and horses, but I knew the loss of Blue Ben would make things dangersome for everyone, but mostly Tom Griffin.

"Is that . . . ?" Mr. Pierce began.

"Yes, sir," I replied. "What's left of him anyway."

He cussed, kicked, and stormed around camp, screeching like one of those steam-powered organs aboard a steamboat, before stopping and staring at me.

"Whose herd stampeded first? You learned that?"

Well, I had, and though I hated to answer the question, I had to.

Mr. Pierce cursed Tom Griffin's name long and hard, then he

ordered Clete and me to ride out and inform every trail boss, every wrangler, every belly-cheater and drover that there would be a funeral on the banks of the Red River shortly after dawn, and he would take it personal if they didn't show up.

"Jack," he called out as I swung into my saddle.

"Tell Tom Griffin if he comes to Blue Ben's funeral, I'll kill him. His men are welcome, but he isn't, not by a damned sight."

"Yes, sir."

It was a mighty fine funeral. Mr. Pierce read from the Good Book, and though I heard some grumbling among the drovers and trail bosses, you can bet your boots no one bellyached within Mr. Pierce's earshot.

We threw up a cross over Blue Ben's grave, then moved out to try to separate the herds and get across the Red River again. That took a spell, ten days about if I recollect right. It took Tom Griffin even longer, only because Mr. Pierce ordered everyone not to assist the Rafter G, that he'd take it as an affront if anyone sided with that killer. For such a rawboned Yankee, Abel Head Pierce threw a lot of weight, especially after what all had happened, and we were halfway to Kansas before Griffin ever got his beef across the Red.

Which could have ended things there, but that incident, Blue Ben's death, but mostly Tom Griffin's refusing to listen to reason, it festered something awful, stuck in Mr. Pierce's craw, and he wouldn't let it pass. Blue Ben was dead, but that wasn't half of it. We had lost better than two hundred head in the stampede—more than seven thousand dollars at market price that year—and Mr. Pierce is a man who likes his money.

We sold our herds in Abilene, sent most of the boys back home, while Mr. Pierce and I waited at the Drover's Cottage for the Rafter G cattle to arrive. I remember sitting in the lobby, smoking a cigar, when a weary, ragged Tom Griffin walked inside and asked for a room.

"I'm sorry," the clerk told him. "We're full up."

That was a lie, and Tom Griffin knew it.

"Do you know who I am?" he asked.

"Yes, sir. But we're still full up."

"I've been bringing my beef to Abilene for four years. I've done business . . ." When he spotted Mr. Pierce, leaning against the balustrade, saw that laughter in Mr. Pierce's cold eyes, Tom Griffin left. He bunked that summer in his cow camp, and approached every cattle buyer in town, only to hear the same story. The summer crept by. September came and went, and the season ended, but Tom Griffin's longhorns remained camped outside town. Finally, he summoned enough courage, or swallowed down his pride, to brace Mr. Pierce at the Bull's Head Saloon.

"Listen, Shanghai," he said, "I was wrong at Red River Crossing, and I'm sorry about all that happened. I'm sorry about ol' Blue. Know he'd been with you for years, but . . . I ain't one to beg, sir, but I got a wife and two little girls, been on tick for so long . . . well, what do you want from me?"

"You want to sell your damned herd?" Mr. Pierce asked.

"You know I have to."

"Then I'll buy them from you, Tom. Ten dollars a head."

Tom Griffin looked as if he'd been gutshot, and that bucket of blood turned quieter than a church on Monday morning.

"I could get better than that in Texas," Griffin said.

"But you aren't in Texas, Tom. And if you want to wait out the winter here . . ."

Everybody in Abilene knew that Tom Griffin had tried to wait out the winter the previous year, hoping for a better price, but that winter had been a hard one, and Tom Griffin's luck turned south. He had lost half his herd, sold out at a loss, forced to limp his way back to Matagorda County on tick and try again that spring. Griffin's face reddened, but he didn't lash out at Mr. Pierce, just stormed through the saloon doors.

We didn't see him again till November, when, hat in hand, he approached Mr. Pierce over breakfast.

"I'll take that offer," he said humbly. "At least I can pay off my crew, pay some of my bills, and get home to my family. Ten dollars a head, and I have fifteen hundred beeves, sir."

"Tom," Mr. Pierce said. "That was the price in October. The price today is eight dollars a head, if I like the way they look."

"I'd go broke selling out for that," Griffin snapped.

"You are broke, Tom. And you'll go broker waiting for a better offer in Abilene." Mr. Pierce's grin wasn't pleasant. "Word is the civic leaders don't want our business anymore. Abilene will be closed to the Texas trade come spring. Now, if you want to risk another winter, Tom, maybe you can push what's left of your beef to Ellsworth next year. If you can afford to pay any drovers or find anyone willing to work for you. Eight dollars, Tom. Cash money. Twelve thousand dollars. But if you wait till tomorrow, the price will be seven."

"You're one son of a bitch, Shanghai Pierce," Tom Griffin said through a tight jaw.

"Tell that to Blue Ben," he answered coolly.

Well, Tom Griffin sold his herd to Mr. Pierce that morning, who, in turn, found a buyer from a Kansas City packing plant willing to pay him $35.75 a head. By then, Griffin had ridden back to Texas, hoping he could make things right come next spring, but Mr. Pierce kept thinking ahead. Come roundup time, you couldn't find a *vaquero* or any man in South Texas fool enough to sign on with the Rafter G. We blackballed Tom Griffin, made him a man alone, and that's when I guess he started pulling the cork. I had never known Tom Griffin to take a drink, but after the spring of 1872 I seldom saw him sober.

Eventually, Mrs. Griffin took the two girls and moved back to her mother's in Sedalia, and Chemical National Bank took over the Rafter G. Shortly afterward I heard rumors that Mrs. Griffin had hired a rich Missouri lawyer, saying she'd rather live with the shame of divorce than be married to a worthless drunk. That's when Tom Griffin drifted to our camp one evening, asked if he could hire on for the drive, which had to make Griffin, in his cups or not, disgusted with himself. Mr. Pierce obviously enjoyed the opportunity to reply that he didn't hire walking whiskey vats to do a man's work. Tom Griffin rode back to the nearest saloon, and, by the time Mr. Pierce and I returned from Wichita that August, Tom Griffin had left the country.

That, also, might have ended things, but the next year, just by chance, we ran into Tom Griffin in Hot Springs, Arkansas. His hair had turned white, his eyes rimmed red, but he looked quite happy when the two of us walked into the Avance Hotel.

"Well, Mister Pierce," he said pleasantly, "Mister Street, do you have reservations with us?"

"You own this place, Griffin?" Pierce asked.

That brought a frown to the Texian's face, and he looked down at the ledger, mumbling something about reservations. Griffin, who once ran thousands of head over several sections of the best country a body could find in Matagorda County, wasn't anything more than a clerk.

"I damn sure want a room," Mr. Pierce said, "so hand over a key, boy."

Color returned to Griffin's face, and he looked up. "I'm sorry, gentlemen, but without a reservation, I can't help you. We're full up. Remember?"

Vengeance, I thought, recalling that time at the Drover's Cottage in Abilene, but Tom Griffin underestimated Abel Head Pierce, who stormed directly into the manager's office.

"Do you own this pigsty?" Mr. Pierce asked.

"Uh . . . I . . . well, only a half-interest, sir."

"How much to buy you out?"

"Sir?"

"You heard me. How much?"

"Mister Pierce, why, well, I couldn't take less than fifteen thousand dollars. This is—"

"Done."

I helped guide the stunned part-owner of the hotel to the bank—Mr. Pierce, naturally, rode—and there we recorded the transaction, and afterward returned to the Avance, where Mr. Pierce grabbed the key to a suite and another key to the adjoining room for me. When Griffin started to protest and threaten to alert the local constabulary, Mr. Pierce waved the duly noted deed in his face.

"I think I can take any room I want since I own this place, Tom."

Griffin's face turned ashen, and like a rooster, Mr. Pierce strutted up the stairs, stopping at the landing and calling down, "Tom?"

Meekly, the man looked up, steeling himself for the words he knew were coming.

"You're fired."

Well, we didn't cross Tom Griffin's trail again for years. I had almost forgotten all about him until this saddle tramp showed up at our camp on the Brazos in the spring of 1884 when we were pushing a herd of two-year-olds to Dodge City by way of the cutoff.

"You looking for a job?" I asked. "Or just riding the grub line?"

Shorthanded as we were after losing a couple boys to bad water, I felt so desperate I figured that bearded wreck of a man could at least ride drag for us.

Staring at me over his plate of beans, he wiped gravy with a frayed sleeve, and said, "Was . . . till I recognized your road brand."

That's when I saw the man for who he was.

"Griffin?"

The dog started barking, and my stomach knotted as Mr. Pierce and Blue Ben II strode into camp, the pup just a nipping at Mr. Pierce's heels. Without a word, Tom Griffin, joints creaking, rose, dropped plate, fork, and coffee cup in the wreck pan, and headed toward his mount.

"Hold up there, cowboy!" Mr. Pierce called to the man's back, and, to the dog, "Stay, Blue, stay."

Well, the dog didn't stay put at all, and when Tom Griffin turned around, Mr. Pierce recognized him immediately. Tom Griffin's hand dropped to his gun, but he was shaking so bad, I knew he wouldn't pull it.

"Griffin! By the saints, I thought you were dead." Mr. Pierce almost doubled over laughing, but he straightened and his face went cold when Tom Griffin spoke quietly.

"I am dead, Shanghai. You killed me years ago. And because of what?" He pointed at the pup, the spitting image of ol' Blue Ben who had been killed at Red River Crossing back in '71. "Because I got that damned dog of yours killed in a stampede? I didn't start the stampede, Shanghai. It was an accident. Still, I took responsibility for it, but you couldn't let that lie, could you? I lost my wife. My girls. My ranch. My damned dignity. Because of a dog?"

Still shaking, Tom Griffin spun, making a beeline for the remuda.

Blue Ben II began barking, and, to our surprise, took off

chasing that old cowhand.

"He's right, Mister Pierce," I said to my boss's back.

"Like hell."

"You never cared one whit about that dog," I reminded him, "till he got killed."

"Maybe, but that son of a bitch over yonder cost me seven thousand dollars, Jack. I haven't forgotten that, even after thirteen years."

"No, sir, but I figure Tom Griffin's paid that debt. With interest."

Mr. Pierce looked at me for what seemed the longest time, and his face softened a bit before he strode away, calling out again, "I said hold up there, cowboy!"

Well, much to my surprise, Mr. Pierce offered Tom Griffin a job, riding drag maybe, but a job, at thirty a month and a bonus at Dodge City. Even more shocking, Griffin took the offer. He said something to me, a few weeks later, that all he had ever known really was cattle, all he ever wanted to do was ranch and cowboy, and now, after thirteen years, he had that chance again. He promised he wouldn't let Shanghai Pierce down.

Yes, he was a broken man by then. Mr. Pierce had broken him; yet, I thought, Mr. Pierce was coming around, mellowing a bit. Besides, Blue Ben II took a shine to Tom Griffin. Every morning we'd find that blue-tick pup curled up in Griffin's sugans, and Ol' Griff would feed that obnoxious little dog breakfast and supper. They became something of a fixture on that drive.

We pushed the herd up to Red River Crossing, and that's when it happened again. Another stampede, only there weren't dozens of herds and 60,000 cattle around, just our own. A lightning strike sent the herd thundering right through camp, wrecked the hoodlum wagon, turned over the chuck wagon, maimed fifteen horses, and killed twenty-one head of cattle before we got them turned and milling.

I'm still not sure how it happened, how he did it, or even why, but we found Tom Griffin's crushed body back in camp, near the blackjacks and smoldering cookfire. The best we could figure it is that Tom, who had been night-herding, had dived off his horse, or maybe it had stumbled, but he had picked up that quivering little puppy, frightened half to death, and tossed it clear of the stampeding cattle. Tom Griffin had saved Blue Ben II's life, even if it had cost him his own.

He wasn't dead when we found him, but I knew he wouldn't last long, not with death's rattle in his throat, not as busted up as his innards had to be. He asked to see Mr. Pierce, his voice stronger than it rightfully should have, and while Sourdough Frankie searched desperately for a bottle of rye in the ruined chuck wagon, Mr. Pierce knelt beside the dying cowhand, cradling the dog in his hands.

"Shanghai," Tom Griffin said, "you want to tell me something?"

"I sure do, Tom," Mr. Pierce said, but Tom Griffin died before Abel Head Pierce could say anything else. He sat there for the longest time, the puppy whimpering in his arms, the only sound around. Finally, seeing the boys worried, restless, and confused, and Mr. Pierce apparently badly shaken, I announced that we'd bury Tom Griffin at Red River Crossing and Sourdough Frankie would carve his name on a piece of board from the destroyed hoodlum wagon.

"No." Mr. Pierce placed the dog on Tom Griffin's chest. Stiffly, he rose and looked every mother's son of us in the eye. "We're taking him to Dodge. Tom Griffin will finish the drive, by thunder, and we'll give him a funeral to remember him by."

Well, Mr. Pierce is a man of his word, so once we had outfitted ourselves, we salted down Tom Griffin's broken body in a coffin Mr. Pierce bought in Spanish Fort, loaded him in the hoodlum wagon, and hauled him to Dodge. Our drovers didn't care much for that at all—coffins and dead bodies giving even the strongest cowboy a bad feeling—but they knew better than to complain or quit on Shanghai Pierce. No one talked about our odd cargo, and we covered the rest of the trail without incident.

Once in Dodge City, after selling the herd and paying off the crew, Mr. Pierce gave us instructions that we would all attend Tom Griffin's funeral and whoever didn't show up would rue the day. The service would begin at 9 o'clock sharp at the Union Church, and by 8:55 that morning every drover we had stood in his Sunday best, which they had bought for the funeral, and hat in hand. A few had brought along their whores, just to increase the turnout.

"This is not worth a tinker's damn," Mr. Pierce told the parson. "Tom Griffin's funeral will draw more than a dozen thirty-a-month drovers, by God, and three chippies."

The parson nodded, and the funeral was put on hold. To hell with the town ordinance prohibiting the packing of firearms, Mr. Pierce told us, so we outfitted ourselves, mounted up, and rode through Dodge, rounding up every person who dared open a door or walk the streets. Mr. Pierce even persuaded the city and Ford County peace officers to help bring crowds out to see Tom Griffin off to Glory.

Better than a thousand people packed the Union Church and crowded several blocks around to hear the sky pilot say a few words and the choir sing a couple of nice hymns. Then—I served as a pallbearer—we walked Tom Griffin, the old coffin we had bought in Spanish Fort replaced by a beautiful one that the undertaker swore would last a century, to Prairie Grove Cemetery, and I'll be damned if the mourners didn't follow us there.

Trailing the pallbearers and coffin, Mr. Pierce led a riderless black horse, one boot placed backward in the stirrup, and a

whore, dressed in white except for a black armband, carried
that yipping little puppy dog, Blue Ben II, in her arms.

With ropes, we lowered Tom Griffin's oak casket into the
grave, tossed some wildflowers on it, and stepped back to hear
Abel Head Pierce address the crowd and, after thirteen years,
make his peace with Tom Griffin.

Or so I thought.

Well, like I said, if you've ever met Abel Head Pierce, you
know he's a hard man, and not always fair-minded. Honest,
certainly, but in forty-odd years I've never known him to own
up to a mistake. The closest he ever came to admitting he was
wrong happened at Prairie Grove Cemetery in Dodge City,
Kansas, in July of 1884, but instead of apologizing, instead of
praising Tom Griffin, he kept his eulogy short.

"Ladies and gentlemen," he said in that abrasive voice, "we're
here to bury Tom Griffin, a drover my *segundo*, Jack Street,
hired for some damned reason. Because, Christ a'mighty, this
dumb son of a bitch that we're burying didn't have brains
enough to stay in his damned saddle. Instead of trying to save
my cattle, hell, he figured to spare the life of this stupid mongrel.
It cost him his life, and me fifteen horses, twenty-one head of
prime beef, a hoodlum wagon, chuck wagon, and four extra
days at Red River Crossing. One thousand, three hundred,
twenty-two damned dollars and seventeen cents, Lord a'mighty.
Tom Griffin, you ignorant bastard, rot in Hell. Now let's all
head over to the Long Branch for a morning bracer. Amen."

Say what you will about Mr. Pierce—likely, I have heard it
already—and while he is contrary, abrasive, and ruthless, I think
there was more to that eulogy than slander and sacrilege. The
Dodge City newspapers all ran front-page articles about Tom
Griffin's funeral—proclaiming it bigger even than Marshal Ed
Masterson's back in '78—although none printed any of Mr.

Pierce's salty language, and that story spread all across Kansas, even on to Missouri and down in Texas. What's more, fourteen years have passed, but you'll still find folks from Dodge to San Antonio who remember Tom Griffin, not as a run-down drunk, but as a cowboy who died under the hoofs. Maybe they don't know what happened in 1871, a lot of them laugh about Mr. Pierce's graveside tirade, but mostly they recall that Tom Griffin gave his life for a dog, which sets pretty high among most folks. His marble tombstone still stands at Prairie Grove Cemetery, and the epitaph "Here Lies A Cowhand"—on Mr. Pierce's dime, though he'll never say so—hasn't faded, which is more than you can say about most drovers' graves. Old trail hands still tell big windies about Tom Griffin, and that's something you can attribute to Abel Head Pierce.

He didn't apologize, not exactly, but that's as close as you'll ever hear one whispered from Mr. Pierce's lips.

PUBLISHING HISTORY

The Antioch County All-Star Game appears for the first time. © 2022 by Johnny D. Boggs.

The Barber of Florence appears for the first time. © 2022 by Johnny D. Boggs.

Blue Norther first appeared in *Tucumcari Literary Magazine*. © 1990 by Johnny D. Boggs.

The Cobbler of Spanish Fort appears for the first time. © 2022 by Johnny D. Boggs.

The Cody War first appeared in *Lost Trails* (Pinnacle Books). © 2007 by Johnny D. Boggs.

Comanche Camp at Dawn first appeared in *Nocona Burgess: The American Indian Cowboy* (Nocona Burgess/Giacobbe-Fritz Fine Art). © 2016 by Johnny D. Boggs.

Crawford McGee first appeared in *Read Me*. © 1990 by Johnny D. Boggs.

Gun on the Wall first appeared in *Dan River Anthology*. © 1990 by Johnny D. Boggs.

Electric Fences first appeared in *The Village Idiot*. © 1992 by Johnny D. Boggs.

I am Hugh Gunter first appeared in *Rough Country* (High Hill Press). © 2013 by Johnny D. Boggs.

Irish Whiskey first appeared in *Portfolio* (University of South Carolina). © 1984 by Johnny D. Boggs.

Massacre at Chest of Drawers Mountain first appeared in *The News & Observer* (Raleigh, North Carolina) (April 30, 2000). ©

2022 by Johnny D. Boggs.

A Piano at Dead Man's Crossing first appeared in *American West: Twenty New Stories from the Western Writers of America* (Forge Books). © 2001 by Johnny D. Boggs.

Plantin' Season first appeared in *Cactus Country: An Anthology of All Things Western, Volume 1* (Cactus Country Publishing). © 2011 by Johnny D. Boggs.

Red River Crossing first appeared in *The Best Stories of the American West, Volume I* (Forge Books). © 2007 by Johnny D. Boggs.

The San Angela Stump Match of 1876 first appeared in *West Texas Lore & Legend* (Permian Basin Bookies). © 2017 by Johnny D. Boggs.

The Snoring Man first appeared in *Red Herring Mystery Magazine*. © 1994 by Johnny D. Boggs.

The Time We Buried Caleb Ketchum first appeared in *Broken Dreams* (Northwoods Press). © 1992 by Johnny D. Boggs. © 2022 by Johnny D. Boggs for restored material.

Umpire Colt first appeared in *Showdown* (High Hill Press). © 2016 by Johnny D. Boggs.

The Water Bearer first appeared in *Boys' Life*. © 2007 by Johnny D. Boggs.

When I Rode with the Boys first appeared in *Ellen: A Collection of Stories and Essays in Honor of Ellen Gray Massey* (Progreso). © 2015 by Johnny D. Boggs.

ABOUT THE AUTHOR

Nine-time Spur Award winner **Johnny D. Boggs** is a recipient of the Western Writers of America's 2020 Owen Wister Award for Lifetime Contributions to Western Literature.

The employees of Five Star Publishing hope you have enjoyed this book.

Our Five Star novels explore little-known chapters from America's history, stories told from unique perspectives that will entertain a broad range of readers.

Other Five Star books are available at your local library, bookstore, all major book distributors, and directly from Five Star/Gale.

Connect with Five Star Publishing

Visit us on Facebook:
  https://www.facebook.com/FiveStarCengage

Email:
  FiveStar@cengage.com

For information about titles and placing orders:
  (800) 223-1244
  gale.orders@cengage.com

To share your comments, write to us:
  Five Star Publishing
  Attn: Publisher
  10 Water St., Suite 310
  Waterville, ME 04901